THE LIFE AND TIMES OF MAJOR FICTION

BOOKS BY JONATHAN BAUMBACH

The Life and Times of Major Fiction

My Father More or Less

The Return of Service

Chez Charlotte and Emily

Babble

Reruns

What Comes Next

A Man to Conjure With

The Landscape of Nightmare

THE LIFE

AND TIMES

OF MAJOR

FICTION

STORIES BY JONATHAN BAUMBACH

FICTION COLLECTIVE

NEW YORK

BOULDER

Acknowledgement is made to the following publications in which
these stories first appeared: *Antaeus* for "Familiar Games," "The
Dinner Party," and "The Life and Times of Major Fiction;" *The Iowa
Review* for "Mother and Father;" *The Mississippi Review* for "Who
Shall Escape Whipping." *The New York Arts Journal* for "The
Honest Company," and "How You Play the Game;" *The North
American Review* for "A Famous Russian Poet," and "Passion?" *The
Seattle Review* for "Children of Divorced Parents," and "The Life of
the President;" *Statements II* for "The Great Cape Cod Shock Scare;"
Pacific Review for "Mr. and Mrs. McFeeley at Home and Away;"
and *Canto* for "The Errant Melancholy of Twilight."

Published by the Fiction Collective with assistance from the National
Endowment for the Arts; the support of the Publications Center,
University of Colorado, Boulder; and the cooperation of Brooklyn
College, Illinois State University and Teachers & Writers Collabora-
tive.

Grateful acknowledgement is made to the Graduate School, the
School of Arts and Sciences, and the President's Fund of the University of Colorado, Boulder.

Library of Congress Cataloging in Publication Data

Baumbach, Jonathan
   The Life and Times of Major Fiction.
I. Title
PS 3552.A844A6   1986   813.'54   86-29215
ISBN: 0-932-51108-2

Typeset by Bytheway Typesetting Services, Inc.
Manufactured in the United States of America
Designed by Abe Lerner

FOR NICO

CONTENTS

FAMILIAR

GAMES

Every family has its games. Ours were in the service of an ostensibly competitive hierarchy. We had to defeat our mother — the game was basketball in those days — before we got to play our father. Not that we got to play him after that either, but if we were ever to play him, the obstacle of our mother had first to be set aside.

Our mother was usually too busy to play, and sometimes too busy to discuss her busyness, though one suspected that she practiced on the sly. If her form was wanting, or subtly underdeveloped, she had an uncanny knack for putting the ball through the hoop from the oddest angles. She played, whenever she could be enticed into a game, in an apron and slippers, and at times, when coming directly from the kitchen, in rubber gloves.

She gave advice while we played, suggestions for improvement, a woman with a pedagogic bent.

The game I most remember is not one of mine but a game my younger brother played against Mother. Phil had challenged me first, but for some reason — perhaps because I thought he might be able to take me — I declined the contest. Having limited natural ability, Phil practiced at every opportunity, studied self-improvement. One could wake up at two A.M., look out the window, and see him taking shots in the dark. His tenacity awed me.

Our mother was not awed. "This will have to be quick,"

she said, making the first basket before Phil could ready himself on defense. "There's something in the oven that needs basting."

"Did that count?" Phil asked, withholding strenuous complaint, not wanting to provoke her into resigning from the game, one of the lessons by example she occasionally offered.

"I'll do that over," Mother said. "You weren't ready."

Phil insisted that it was all right, that even had he been fully prepared he couldn't have stopped her shot.

Phil took the ball out at the crest of the driveway, which was approximately thirty-five feet from a basket hung on a wooden backboard from the top of our garage, dribbled to the left, then to the right, then to the left again, proceeding by degrees to an advantageous spot. Our mother waited for him, unmoving, at the foul line, her arms out.

Mother blocked Phil's first shot, knocking it behind him. Phil ran down the ball and resumed his pattern of moving ostentatiously from side to side. He told me later that his idea was to get Mother to commit herself.

It was Mother's policy to treat Phil's feints and flourishes as invisible gestures. The more Phil flashed about, showcasing his skills, the more unblinkingly stationary Mother became. Phil's brilliant maneuvering tended to cancel itself out and he invariably ended up coming right to Mother, shooting the ball despairingly against her outstretched hand.

"That's not getting you anywhere," she told him.

That knowledge had already inescapably reached Phil, and one could tell he was planning new strategy, though at the same time he also wanted to demonstrate that his original plan of attack was not without merit. He was down three baskets to none before he decided to relinquish his exquisite shuffle and shoot from the outside.

Phil sinks his first long shot and Mother's lead falls to two.

2

I've neglected to mention procedure, assuming mistakenly that we all play this game in the same way. In our rules, the player that has been scored upon gets the ball out, which tends to keep the games closely contested. Not always. If Phil is to catch up, it will be necessary for Mother to miss at least two more opportunities.

It is Phil's strategy to force Mother to shoot her odd shot from just beyond her range. He presses her when she takes the ball out, swiping at it repeatedly, on occasion slapping her hands.

"I don't enjoy that," she complains. "I don't think it's very nice."

Phil apologizes and steps back, giving Mother the breathing room she needs to launch her two-handed shot. One of its peculiarities is that when it leaves her hands it never seems to be moving in the direction of the basket. In its earliest stages, the poorly launched missile seems fated to fall short and to one side, an embarrassing failure. Halfway in its course, the ball seems buoyed by an otherwise unnoticed wind and accrues the remote chance of reaching the front or side of the rim. The shot outlasts expectation, gains momentum in flight, and instead of touching the front of the rim, lifts over it, ticks the back rim, echoes off the front, and drops through. For an opponent to watch the flight of one of Mother's shots is to risk heartbreak.

Phil has seen Mother's game before and is no longer as vulnerable to the disappointment that comes of false expectation.

"That's a terrific shot," says Phil, hitting one of his own as Mother basks in the compliment.

Unharried by Phil, Mother misses high off the backboard, the shot extending itself beyond the call of accuracy. Phil takes the rebound and dribbles into the corner.

"That must be very tiring," says his stationary opponent. "I don't think you ought to waste so much motion."

Phil takes a jump shot from the corner and cuts the deficit to one. It is a shot he has rehearsed, though he shakes his head as if blessed by undeserved fortune.

"That was a beauty," Mother says, pretending as she does disinterest in the outcome. She shuffles into position to launch her shot, Phil crowding her, waving his arms. Suddenly, accelerating the pace of her shuffle, she goes by him, a move neither Phil nor I have witnessed before. She lays the ball in off the backboard, though it characteristically revolves around the rim a few times before dropping.

Phil, one can tell, is dismayed, has his mind on defending against Mother's next shot instead of readying himself for his own. A halfhearted jump shot falls short and rolls out of bounds. Mother's ball.

Leading six baskets to four, Mother refuses her advantage, or gives that appearance, hefting her odd heave with more than usual indifference, the ball missing long and to the left. "What was I thinking of?" she says to herself.

One is never sure whether it is generosity or tactic.

Phil matches Mother's indifference with a shot even further off the mark than its predecessor.

"Are you letting me win?" Mother asks.

It is only after Mother hits her next shot, a casual two-hander that bounds in off the backboard, that Phil is able to regain his touch.

"You may have made that one, but you're rushing your shot," Mother tells him.

Phil says it's not so.

"Believe what you like," says Mother. "I'm only telling you what I know to be true."

"Why don't you give me the credit of knowing what I'm doing?" says Phil.

While this argument is going on, Mother sinks another long shot, increasing her lead to three baskets.

Showing off, Phil dribbles under the basket and lays the ball in from behind his ear.

4

Our mother claps her hands in appreciation. "That maneuver, if maneuver is the word for it, took my breath away," she says.

The score at this point—I am serving as scorekeeper for the match—is eight baskets for Mother, six for Phil. The first player to reach twelve, while being at least two baskets ahead, is the victor.

Although comfortably in the lead, Mother appears disconsolate, nudging the ball in front of her with the toe of her slipper.

"What's the matter?" Phil asks her.

"Who said anything was the matter?"

Phil is momentarily defeated by Mother's question, gives his opponent considerable space for her next shot.

She takes her time, holding the ball out toward Phil, teasing him with its proximity. "Aren't you playing?" she asks him.

"Take your shot, okay?"

"I'm waiting for you, big shot," she says, dandling the ball. "You're not guarding me the right way."

Phil inches closer, waves an arbitrary hand in the direction of the ball.

And still Mother refuses to launch her shot.

"What have I done wrong?" Phil wants to ask. I know the feeling, have been trapped in similar mystifications.

Mother sits on the ground, her arms crossed in front of her. Phil, not to be put in the wrong, follows suit. The progress of the game has been temporarily halted.

Mother gets up after a while and announces that she is willing to continue if Phil is willing to apologize for his misbehavior.

Phil says he's sorry, says it two or three times since, as it appears, he has no idea what for, and gets to his feet.

Mother scores on a long, unlikely shot that angles in off the backboard. Phil shoots before readying himself and misses to the right, rushing to the basket to retrieve his own rebound. Unguarded, he scores on a lay-up and receives some brief applause from his opponent.

"Thank you one and all," he says, mocking himself, flipping the ball behind his back to our mother.

"I hope you're not trying to impress me," she says, nullifying his basket with one of her own.

Phil dribbles behind his back, through his legs, whirling and turning, exhausting his small repertoire of tricks before kicking the ball out of bounds.

When in the course of her deceptively effective performance Mother reaches eleven baskets, needing only one more to claim victory, she hits a cold spell and misses on her next five attempts. Phil, more by attrition than escalation of skill, gradually edges to one basket behind.

The association comes unbidden and without rational cause. I was in the garden with my mother. We were weeding, or she was; I was watching the process or looking for something to do. There were children in the next yard playing. I could see them, just barely, through the spaces between the slats in their high fence. The game they were playing was like no game I had ever seen before.

There were two of them—at first I thought there were four—a boy and a girl, my age or a year or two older. The girl was taller than the boy and more obviously mature, but girls tend to be more advanced at that age. The reason I didn't know them was that they were new to the neighborhood, their parents—I'm assuming they were brother and sister, though perhaps not—had just bought the house next door.

Did they think the high fence of their garden screened them from the eyes of outsiders? I couldn't imagine what they thought. It may have been they were unconcerned with the opinions of others.

The top half of the girl, at least that, was uncovered and

one of her budlike breasts available to my limited perspective. The other breast, insofar as I could tell, was covered by the back of the dark blond head of the boy. The girl's long hair, raven black, glistening in the sun like wet tar, covered much of her face. The boy seemed to be pecking at her small breast in imitation of a chicken. The girl was laughing, though without sound—at least I heard no sound—her wide mouth appearing periodically through the waterfall of her hair. The boy danced up and down, moving from one foot to the other.

I felt something stiffening against my leg and turned away, turned in a way that protected my secret from the possibility of Mother raising her eyes. The price of my reticence was to give up my view of the game on the other side of the fence. I sensed that Mother was watching me, that she would look up from time to time to see what I was doing, though I never caught her in the act.

When I cautiously returned to my vigil, the picture had changed, took some moments to assimilate in its new form. I blinked my eyes, sucked in my breath.

"What was that?" my mother asked without raising her eyes.

"It wasn't anything," I think I said, not wanting to be heard, not by them, thinking the words rather than saying them.

The first thing I saw was the girl's naked behind thrust out like a thumb, her long hair screening it from full view. She was standing with her legs apart, knees bent, leaning forward. The boy was not where I could see him, not at first. Momentarily, the girl jumped forward, legs askew, as if imitating a frog. Then the boy—he had been somewhere else in the yard—performed a similar jump. I assumed they were playing Follow the Leader or some game of similar principle. It seemed innocent enough except for them both being unclothed and except for the apparent excitement in the air, the sense that they were doing something in violation of the rules. When the girl hopped on her left foot the boy recorded the gesture with his own. Then she hopped on her right foot, as did the boy. Then she did a tumble in the grass, a forward somersault of no special difficulty, though done with exceptional grace. The boy leaned forward to do his, then apparently decided against it. The girl stamped her foot in mock anger, a hand on her hip.

"If you won't do it, you'll have to pay the penalty," I think she said. "And you know what the penalty is, don't you?"

In the next moment she was chasing him around the yard, calling out some threat I couldn't quite hear and was unable to imagine. The word *penalty* was part of it. I could only make out their relative positions when they crossed my line of vision. The boy kept dodging her, putting himself in peril then slipping away.

I heard my mother groan with exhaustion, an oblique request for aid. I was afraid she would see what I was looking at, so I withdrew my eyes, pretended to study the ground.

I went down to my knees, staying as close to the fence as I could without creating attention, and dislodged a handful of weeds and grass.

I was about to glance through the slats when I saw my mother standing over me, her huge shadow preceding her. "Make sure you get the roots," she said. She was there to offer instruction.

While she was there, more shadow than substance, I didn't dare look through the spaces in the fence, though the temptation was extreme. What was the penalty the girl whose name I may have known and have now forgotten intended to exact? My life, I thought at the time, depended on such knowledge.

I pulled the weeds as she advised, thinking if I did it right, she would go away, but she continued to watch and to instruct, though there was no longer any point to her instruction, no longer the slightest need.

"You're doing very nicely," she said, "except some of what you pull out aren't weeds."

"It's like having someone read over your shoulder," I said. "You make me self-conscious. I know what to do. You don't have to watch."

"I know I don't *have* to," she said. "I'm watching because I enjoy watching you weed."

The only way to get her to move away, I thought, was to stop weeding, which I did, announcing I was bored, lying on my back in the grass with my arms out. The sun was hot and I could feel my face burn.

Nothing I did or didn't do would get her to leave. Something astonishing was going on on the other side of the fence, and I was missing it because of Mother's lingering presence. I mentioned that I heard the phone ringing in the house but that didn't move her. I weeded in another part of the garden, thinking she would follow me there to see how I was doing. I was sick with desperation.

She didn't follow, remained standing with her back to the neighbor's high fence, surveying her garden with benign indifference, a permanent obstruction to my hopes.

When Phil tied the game at eleven all, Mother broke her fast and scored on a towering set shot that bounded in off the back rim, the ball in flight for the longest time, seeming to hover over the basket awaiting official clearance to land.

Mother's sudden resurgence of skill seemed to discombobulate Phil who disguised the tension he felt, the sense of impending failure, by becoming silly. He wriggled with mock arrogance as he took out the ball, whistling over and over some mindless jingle from a detergent commercial. You

9

could see he was afraid to let the ball out of his hands. Though our mother gave him ample room, he withheld his shot, edging the ball closer to the basket by degrees. Mother stepped away at his approach, bided her time. I would have called to him to shoot—it was hard to resist—but it wasn't my part. Greedy for better position, Phil forced his way closer, Mother acceding step for step. When he decided he was close enough—he was already under the basket—and sought to reclaim his dribble, the ball glanced off his foot and went out of bounds.

"What bad luck," Mother said.

Phil kicked the ball before turning it over, said he would never play this effing game again, not if his life depended on it.

Mother reprimanded Phil for his poor sportmanship, said it didn't matter who won, it was the fun of the game and what you learned from it that counted.

Phil said if there was any fun in losing, none of it had ever come his way.

Although Phil had in effect conceded defeat, the game had its course to run. Mother had a habit of keeping things going beyond their normal duration.

Clenched with mock determination, Phil crowded Mother as she put the ball in play, waving his arms in her face, goading her with childish taunts. He would not give up the last basket, he was letting us know, without the formality of a struggle. One could see that Mother disapproved of the tactic, thought it excessive or in bad taste. At one point she put down the basketball to shake a finger at him. "Don't make me lose my temper," she warned him.

Phil, his face red, said he was only doing his best and no one could be faulted for that, could they. Could they?

Mother thought this assertion unworthy of a reply.

"Are you ready?" she asked him.

"If you're ready, I am," he said. "I got your number, lady."

In deliberate fashion, Mother feinted to the right and side-stepped to the left, hip to the right, step to the left, shoulder to the left, sidestep to the right.

Phil grudgingly yielded space, side step by side step, the court shrinking on him, his balance confused. Still, he would not let her have her way, not then, not for a moment.

The repetition of her movements would only take her so far and just when we thought she had nowhere to go she surprised us again. In the next moment, or the next, she appeared to take flight, spinning in the direction opposite from the one she had been going, rising from the ground, lifting the ball over her head with two hands as she flew. Neither of us believed what we saw, required at the end the corroboration of the other's witness. Mother, in her apron and house slippers, taking flight, rising to the height of the basket, suspended like disbelief in air, slipping the ball through the rim like a gift, like a secret. Phil stood at her feet and waved, a belated farewell, his mouth agape.

In later years, if one of us derogated her ability, the other would bring up the recollection of her glorious moment as reproof. Mostly, it was as if it had never happened.

Mother circled the basket, keeping her observers in momentary suspense, before donating the ball to the charity of her triumph.

When she returned to the ground she apologized for letting herself get carried away.

Phil fought back tears, offered the hand of a graceful loser.

Mother enthused over the improvement in Phil's game, said that in truth she had been lucky, that Phil would surely win the next time.

Phil, you could tell, was willing to believe her. He was young enough then to trust forever in illusion.

MOTHER AND
FATHER

The Game is Pool, sometimes called eight ball. My father and mother play the game each night before going to bed. I am there as observer, too young to account my age. My father likes to break and my mother, who is new to pool, tends to give the old man his head. It is her habit to admire his every gesture, his hesitations, false starts, benign mischances. Sometimes when he chalks his cue in his unassuming way, she can't help but emit a crow of pleasure at the secret grace of the gesture. Her praise makes him irritable, tends to throw him off his game. "I don't know what's wrong with me," he says when he scratches on the break. "What a stupid thing to do."

My mother allows that there must have been a distracting noise from outside and offers him the occasion to replay the opening hit.

"You usually break so beautifully," she adds. "I can spend whole days just watching you make the break."

"Well, you won't have another chance of watching it today," my father says. "I take full responsibility for my misplays. My failure is already part of the recorded past."

"I don't blame you for saying that," my mother says. "By the way, have you seen my stick? I like, as you know, the little one."

My father hands her his cue, which she accepts for an

12

unhappy moment, then returns. "This is nicer, but I really prefer the one I'm used to."

She goes to the back wall and checks out the four remaining cues, discarding each in turn. "One of them must be yours," my father says, chewing on his impatience. "That's all we have."

Unconvinced, my mother selects the second smallest of the four remaining ones, which is visibly warped and has a worn tip.

"That one's no good," my father says, trying to take it from her. Their struggle produces inertia.

"You never let me use the one I want," my mother says. My father reads the cracks in the ceiling as antidote to that remark.

It is my mother's practice to address the first ball she fixes on and then decide in the ensuing moment that it is not for her. At that point she will ask my father if there is a better shot available, something more in keeping with her limited skill.

Putting symbol ahead of fact, my father denies that there is a shot on the table easier than the one my mother has fixed on. That said, the issue cleared, he manages with undisguised irritation to find her something better.

"I don't know," my mother says, moving between her alternatives, squinting over each as if to estimate its degree of difficulty. "They both look equally hard."

"The one I chose is easier," he insists.

"If you say so," says his skeptical opponent, rushing her shot. She mis-hits the cue ball, sending it in an alternate direction, accidentally nipping the five ball into a side pocket. Elation comes and goes.

"Was that the ball you were shooting?" my father asks.

The question flusters her temporarily. "I don't remember," she says. "Was that the one you recommended?"

My father chalks his cue to occupy an angry heart. "You

13

can have the ball," he says. "All acts include their intentions."

My mother does not want any favors, reclaims the five
from the ball drop and with the best will in the world is
unable to find a place on the table to give it rest.

"I want you to have it," my father says.

"You're too good to me," my mother replies, stuffing the
ball in her apron pocket. With a flourish of determination,
she drops the two in a side pocket and leaves herself in the
worst possible position for a following shot.

"What do I do now, Max?" she asks.

The question does not elicit an answer, perhaps does not
expect one. My mother studies the table as if the geometric
language of the balls were an indecipherable code. If she
doesn't take her shot in the next moment, my father will
break down and tell her all.

My mother chooses the most impossible shot of several
improbable alternatives, reordering the table, and leaving
my father without a shot to call his own.

His chronic irritation rises to the occasion. After circling
the table a few times, he narrowly misses a bank shot on the
ten the laws of physics had denied him in advance.

My mother claps her hands politely, fingers to palm.
"That was almost wonderful," she says.

"It's the story of my life," says my father.

As the game goes on, attrition works its will. Father
moves ahead three balls to two, his first advantage of the
match. My mother rises to the occasion at her next turn
when, her intent elsewhere, she drops two of the solid balls
with a single shot.

"I told you I was better off shooting my way," she says.

My mother's way, let it be said, is notable for having the
cue move tremulously from side to side as it approaches the
cue ball, coming at it from all sides. My father has advised
her to tighten the groove between her fingers, but my moth-

er's success, accidental or not, is dependent on her own method.

My mother mis-hits the one ball into a corner pocket and assumes a five to three advantage.

My father chalks his cue to excess while my mother calculates her next play. As the game progresses, her pace becomes correspondingly deliberate. My father, a man of no patience in the best of seasons, appears on the verge of urging her to get whatever it is over and done.

"I have such trouble choosing my shots," she says in anticipation of his complaint. "Won't you help me just a little bit, Max."

"You're killing me, Helen," he says. "Why should I be complicit in my own defeat." He informs her that the four ball might be gently kissed into a corner pocket.

"The four?" My mother charts the distance with a glance. The ball idles in the foyer of a corner pocket at the far end of the table. "Max, you could make that shot, but I couldn't. Is there anything closer?"

My father says nothing to this, apparently aware that her complaint is obligatory, and hums an idle tune to himself to pass the time.

Sighing at his generosity, she lines up the shot with her characteristic astigmatic perception. (The wobble of her stick, like the blowing of a wind, tends to compensate for the inaccuracy of her aim.)

The cue ball, at my mother's touch, skips across the green in the general direction of its intent, kissing the four ball in such a way as to deny it sanctuary, the white ball visiting the pocket in its place.

"That's what you call a scratch, isn't it?" she asks. My father makes an affirmative noise in his throat. "I knew all along the shot was too long for me."

"You were proven right," my father says.

My mother has difficulty deciding what ball of hers

to return, her fondness for them equal and indiscriminate. "Is the one all right?" she asks, "or must it be the last one I made."

"Anyone," says the authority.

While my mother procrastinates, my father charts the sequence of his remaining three shots, chalking his cue idly.

My mother returns the five, offering an elaborate rationalization for a decision that might have gone several different ways.

Concentrating on getting suitable position for the second of his three shots, or perhaps deflected by the pressures of irritation, my father misses a routine play on the fourteen, which had been lolling just to the right of a side pocket.

My mother is outraged at fate on my father's behalf. "You deserved to make it," she says. "If there was any justice, the ball would have fallen for you."

"Justice wasn't wanting," says her adversary. "Merely skill."

"Well, I thought it was a difficult shot," says my mother, "and that you did beautifully with it." That issue out of the way, she proceeds (who can say how?) to run her next two balls and barely miss a third, leaving her with one solid (the resurrected five) and the eight ball to carry off victory.

Up until this point, my father has not taken her quite seriously as an adversary. It has begun to dawn on him that there is more art in mother's game than accident, or that she is a mistress of benign fortune. He adjusts himself in imperceptible ways to whatever knowledge he is willing to own. Losing is too important to him to accept without a struggle.

Father is responsible for the stripes, the balls from nine through fifteen, the higher denominations, while my mother's province is the solids (balls one through seven). The eight ball, which gives the contest its name, is the final reckoning.

My father has a reasonable shot at the nine ball which resides on the rail some six inches from a corner pocket. To

make the shot he must hit ball and cushion simultaneously
Though margin for error is small, the shot is unambiguous.
My mother leans over his shoulder as he calculates his play,
a student of father's expertise.

"I can't shoot when you sit on my shoulder," he reminds
her.

"Try," she says, teasing. "I bet you can do it if you try."
My father makes the shot without looking back, then makes
another. Anger inspires him.

My mother oohs and ahhs, creating a din of admiration.
"Some days you just don't seem to know how to miss," she
says.

"It happens that you're winning this game," he says.

"That's because I don't play to win," says my mother.
"Winning and losing are the same to me."

"That's a lot of shit if I may say so," says my father,
rushing his shot, cue ball following the twelve into a corner
pocket. He mutters a mild oath, waving an arm as if knocking flies away.

"You ought to be pleased that you made the ball in the
first place, and not always focus on the bad side of things."
"I didn't put enough back spin on the cue ball," he says,
returning the twelve to the designated spot. "It was a failure
of concentration."

My mother misses her next four attempts at the five ball,
misses them badly, insisting with each failure that she plays
the game merely for the pleasure of it. My father, who plays
without pleasure, manages to dispose of the two remaining
stripes and has only the eight ball to put away to claim
victory. The sudden collapse of my mother's small skill trou-
bles him. He suspects her of intentionally letting him win
and is disposed, before taking what could be his final shot,
to inform her of his suspicion.

The charge doesn't surprise my mother and she denies it
categorically without conviction.

17

My father misses a middling difficult bank shot on the eight.

My mother sinks her cue ball in the corner and is obliged to return another of her solids to the table.

"You didn't need to do that," my father says.

"I'm doing the best I can," my mother protests. "I told you I don't care about winning."

The eight ball, my father's final quarry, awaits him in front of the far right corner pocket. There is much green between cue ball and eight, but the shot is less troubling to him than what he takes to be his wife's patronizing play. He hangs up his cue and sits down on a high stool, his arms folded in front of him.

"Aren't you taking your turn?" my mother asks.

"I'm retiring from the fray," says my father. "If I wanted to play solitaire, I wouldn't have engaged an opponent."

"Anyway, you've won the game," she says, offering the hand of a graceful loser.

My father gets off the stool and retrieves his stick. "This is the last time I'm playing with you," he says, "the absolutely last time."

This news ruffles my mother's feathers, though not so my father would notice. She says it's all the same to her whether they play or not, the game childish in her view, puerile, callow, infantile, a primitive pastime.

My father scratches on the eight ball, losing the game.

My mother refuses to claim victory, insists that my father really won, offering him the temptation of a replay. He almost accedes to her offer, rejecting it with visible pain.

When my mother walks off with her unclaimed victory — "You lost, I didn't win," she insists — my father racks the balls for another round.

I watch him from a high stool in the back of the room, his only spectator.

He walks around the table once before chalking his cue,

18

businesslike in his aspect, characteristically harried. Father always looks as if he's trying to remember something he's supposed to do and forgotten.

The white ball explodes off his cue, bears down on the triangulated pack with uncompromising violence, dispersing the balls every which way, banging them about from end to side, three perhaps four balls escaping the table into waiting pockets. In five succeeding turns, six more balls retire from the table, my father announcing their destination before each shot.

Finally, a ball refuses to do as it's told, and my father, who had been moving about the table in a hurry, disappears into the bathroom for some private reckoning. I grow to doubt his return.

He misses twice again before he cleans the table, sinking his final ball by banging it into a corner pocket with self-conscious flourish.

He hangs up his cue, puts out the lamp over the arena, takes one last look over his shoulder, and leaves, some misplaced notes from a song on his tongue.

I remain behind on the higher of the high stools, deserted and forgotten, too small to climb down without aid, a first and final witness.

WHO SHALL

ESCAPE

WHIPPING

Wednesday, 5 October: *Film Staff Meeting at 4. Don't forget flowers. Call L.*

The same cryptic note — Call L — recurs on Thursday, October 6, which opens certain speculations. Did I miss contact with L on Wednesday, or did I simply not get around to calling? The likelihood is that I didn't call, had second thoughts, or was too busy, too involved in my work (I was writing a screenplay, as I remember) to get to the phone. (I've been going through the pages of a 1977 desk calendar, revisiting the events of that year through what seems at times an impenetrable code. I was intending to employ the base for the 1981 filler, but once into 1977 I couldn't turn away.)

It doesn't follow. If the call was important enough to note on the calendar, I would have found the time to bestir myself. It would help, of course, in making sense of what happened if I could remember who L was. I suffer like most people from selective amnesia, forgetting those things that are no pleasure to remember.

There are (or were) thirteen people in my life whose first or last names begin with L. Eight are women; two are former wives.

I remember an occasion when a theater manager whom I considered a friend turned down a play of mine for production, citing reasons that were virtually incoherent. I was driven to call the man up and ask him what he meant by his incomprehensible note. I planned to phone him at his office the next day and perhaps even wrote it down on the calendar as a reminder to myself. The call, despite its reasonableness, embarrassed me, and I put it off, each day's delay increasing my anger, for a period of weeks. When I finally got on the phone, I was so angry I could barely make myself understood. I found myself overstating my case so as to make it impossible for him to take it seriously. "You can't read a word," I shouted at him, and, mortified for us both, he said it was altogether possible that I was right.

Friday, 7 October: *Radio Interview at 12:30. Don't forget to pick up gloves and scarf. Dentist at 3:00.* There is no mention of L, which might mean that the call had been concluded the day before.

There are no pressing obligations on Saturday, 8 October, just the inexplicable message: *Fantasies in present tense like color in a black and white movie.*

I am reminded of a story I had heard about a woman who one day, without apparent warning, asked her husband of sixteen years to move out. She was tired of him, she announced. He cluttered the air with irrelevancies. The man, who couldn't bear to be discarded by his beautiful, celebrated wife—she had a small reputation as a painter of erotic landscapes—offered to change his ways. A truce was negotiated. The woman would see if she could remake this unacceptable husband into the man she imagined she wanted. One of the woman's whims was that her husband dress in woman's clothing before lovemaking. An ordinarily timid man, the husband tended, under provocation, to excessive behavior. After reluctantly taking on his new role, he was continually turning up in some bizarre new costume, offering himself to his wife like a parody of a gift. The woman

21

was moved, despite her contempt, by this new aspect of her husband. She found him more beautiful in his feminine disguise than she had ever thought him before. His nature seemed to redefine itself. He had that insistent glow that many pregnant women have in the early months. His undisguised neediness sometimes brought tears to her eyes. She sketched him, wearing one of her bathrobes, frolicking among goats. Afterward they made love—his reward—on a couch in her studio. Her pleasure in the charade began to stale after a few weeks. There was, after all, something freaky about having a husband disguised as a woman, something deeply unacceptable. And when it came down to it, he was as unimaginative as a woman as he had been as a man.

The husband, whose name I can't remember, whom I think of as H, lamented his failure to please, said he was willing to take full responsibility for the needless disrepair of their marriage. What else might he do to regain his place? he asked.

The woman said she was open to suggestions, though said it in a way that indicated that she couldn't imagine H offering an idea that could possibly engage her. The husband wondered if they couldn't carry their recent experiment one step further as a means of furthering mutual understanding. They would this time move beyond the exchanging of clothes to the transference of identities. He was very sincere about his idea, and the woman, although dubious about the success of such a regimen, consented to try it out for a few days. She didn't want to seem a bad sport, she reported.

It didn't work. They couldn't very well switch identities— at best they played in a superficial way at being the other— and in short order the woman renewed her request that H take his tiresome presence elsewhere. If she were going to be a husband, she decided, the man she lived with was not the role model she wanted to emulate.

Not everything has been tried, said the resourceful H,

some stones that might have been turned remain unturned. The woman was dubious, was ready for a change in her life, but out of guilt or habit (perhaps even love or its memory) offered her husband one last chance to prove himself.

I am trying to understand why in 1977 I was unable to complete a call to someone referred to only as L for a period extending at least a week and probably longer. It might have been that my phone was on the blink. The slightest storm tended that year to put the phone's nose out of joint, though that hardly seems a suitable excuse. The evidence suggests that I resisted making this call, was ambivalent about its necessity.

When I was a kid of sixteen or seventeen, I had great difficulty phoning some girl I hardly knew for a date. I tended to hang around the phone, working up my courage, sometimes dialing all but one of the digits before returning receiver to cradle in defeat. I think it was the prospect of the call that bothered me more than the call itself, the artificial chatter, the inescapable preliminaries. Even then I had no small talk. Sometimes, to avoid embarrassment, I would write out the dialogue in advance, anticipating the girl's responses or overriding them. More often I postponed the call, held onto it for weeks awaiting the propitious moment, which sometimes never came.

I still have difficulties making phone calls to people from whom I want something, resist them tenaciously.

Was the mysterious L expecting this call, anticipating it with pleasure, dreading it? If I knew L were expecting to hear from me, if I were absolutely sure of that, I wouldn't have postponed the call for as long as I had. The prospect of having to identify myself fills me with anxiety.

I am tempted to call the woman with the partially discarded husband, L, which is not her real initial. This somewhat

23

celebrated artist, whom I present in the disguise of L, gives her unsatisfactory husband one final chance to regain his lost tenure in her life. "I'm listening," she says, hands on hips. He will do absolutely anything she asks of him, he says, *absolutely* anything. It takes a while for the implications of this to register.

"This is laughable," she says, not so much laughing as smiling broadly, fingering the idea in her imagination. "Even if I were willing to go along with the idea, which I happen to think is obscene, how can such an arrangement be enforced?" H has an answer to that too. She can whip him if he fails to carry out the least of her directives. He throws open the foyer closet door to reveal what looks like a coiled snake.

L says she will stay with H for a trial period if he will agree in writing to be ruled by her decisions. If he fails to obey her, or fails to please her by his obedience, he is to be punished at her whim. They giggle like witches around a cauldron as the agreement is drawn up. "I think I might begin to love you again," she says.

Would she really have the nerve to whip him, L wondered, if H did something that displeased her? How could he avoid it? It was in her nature to be easily displeased.

For a time, to threaten him with the whip, to tickle his back with its tentacle was sufficient retribution. H would cower and cringe with exaggerated dismay. And L would extort a promise from him not to displease her again. "You know what's going to happen to you if you do it again," she'd say. It was hard to make these solemn threats while keeping a straight face, though L had a certain self-control. Only an occasional giggle would escape like a hiccough or a belch. H, on the other hand, would be overwhelmed with hilarity, crying and laughing and pleading for mercy all at once. It was a heady game for a while.

L has gotten bored with the unimaginative quality of H's servility. It has become necessary for the life of the senses to draw a little blood. One evening after he has broken a dish cleaning up, L cuts her husband's face with the whip. H cries out in real pain, his hand over his eye.

The celebrated painter of erotic landscapes is all repentence and tears. "Let your mistress kiss it," she says. "Oh my sweet thing, my dearest, my darling." Tenderness moves up or down the scale (depending on your measure) to passion. They make love on the dining room floor with a clamor that causes a hand-painted plate to fall from the mantle. "You can't make a marriage without breaking a few plates," says H. It is the kind of dense remark that makes the woman want to whip him again and again.

I have gone another week without calling the L on my calendar, have forgotten L or renounced the idea for unremembered reasons. On October 19, it says: *Don't forget tense shift.* It was a note to myself about a story I was in the middle of writing, a reminder to put fantasies in the present tense. If I can trust my recollection on the matter, I rejected that advice to myself and kept fantasies and nonfantasies alike in the conventional past. The advice was written on the calendar not to be taken but to be exorcised as a possibility. Maybe the charge to phone L had a similar intent. Maybe the repeated reminder was a way of canceling out the necessity of the call, a game I played with myself on some unconscious level.

And why should I have wanted to avoid calling? The same question repeats itself. The same answer comes to mind: I was protecting myself from some form of rejection. Even now, three years later, the idea of being refused by L enrages me. It follows, I suspect, that the reason I can't remember L's identity is that I can't forgive her (his?) probable rejection of my request. What an agony of unresolved obsession. Unable to ask for something I want, I blame the person I am too reticent to approach for an uncommitted slight.

There it is on Tuesday, November 1. *Call L.* More than three weeks have passed since its first appearance on my calendar, and the need for communication with L persists like an unhealed sore.

The other L was upset with herself for letting H provoke her into violence. "I won't whip you again," she told him, "not until I recover from the sense of revulsion I have at my own behavior." H sulked at the rebuke, broke another dish, seeking to provoke. "You bastard," she whispered to him. She considered asking him to leave, though thought the timing inappropriate.

They didn't talk through dinner, barely looked at one another, and afterward sat apart in the living room reading separate copies of the same book.

"You're being terribly provocative," she whispered.

"You know what you can do," he said, pointing to the whip, which was lying on the rug like a coiled serpent.

"Never again," she said.

H removed his Italian shirt and tossed it on the floor.

L sighed. "You have a beautiful back," she said as a matter of unassailable fact. "It was never your back that displeased me."

He wore the shirt over his shoulders like a cape, then slipped it off in slow motion as if he were doing a burlesque number. "It awaits your pleasure, mistress," he said. L returned to her book.

H had the sense that she was watching him while pretending to read. After a while he took off his pants and folded them neatly over the arm of the couch on which L sat with an open book in her lap.

"I wish you would stop whatever you think you're doing," she whispered, regretting the remark the moment it was spoken.

He had difficulty reading her, though pretended to impressive self-assurance. "Is that an order or a suggestion?" he asked.

She was tempted to pick up the whip and lash him for his dullness, but instead stifled a yawn.

"I give you fair warning I'm not going to stop," he said.

It was not what she wanted—how tiresome everything was!—though she was intrigued by the tenacity of his failure. H was touching in his foolishness. She glanced up from her book, paid brief notice to his position in the room. As she had no response to him, none large enough to matter, she felt constrained to invent one. "You promised to do anything I asked," she said. "Isn't that so? Absolutely anything and without question."

H stood alluringly in his shorts, hands on hips. "Have I been unfaithful?"

"I don't want to see you again for the rest of the day," she said. "I want you out of my sight."

He looked injured, though offered no argument, no request for reprieve. He picked up the whip, wrapped it around his neck like a scarf and left the room with as much dignity as a man dressed solely in undershorts and socks could affect.

His absence brought tears to her eyes, a combination of shame and anger. Who was he to walk out on her that way? Her heart was beating violently. She thought how awful she had been to him and how awful he was to have allowed her to be so awful. She thought of going after him and saying she was sorry and ordering him to return. I am guessing at her thoughts. The fact is, after a suitable hiatus, she got up from her place on the couch and went looking for her exiled husband. She found him sitting in a yoga posture in front of the cat's dish. "How terrible I've been to you," she said, and knelt next to him. It was as though the cat's dish were some kind of sacred object to which they both paid obeisance.

Eventually, they moved into the baby-sitter's narrow bed and made love with what L refers to as "heart-rending tenderness." Details are left to the imagination. What we do know is that H achieved a temporary restoration and that L grieved for several days at the treatment the man had suffered at her hand.

On November 2, I note that I finished Nabokov's *Despair*. I started the book in 1975 at the recommendation of a former editor, read twenty-five pages, then succeeded in losing the book on the subway. A woman dropped a glove on my lap without my noticing. When she reclaimed the glove in a hurried gesture she picked up the book, which was under it, stuffing both in her purse and rushing out of the train. That's my story about *Despair*.

There it is on November 3: "Don't forget to call L!" As if a failure of memory were the issue. Anyway the warning was there. I was not to forget. How did I get around calling this time. I called when L was out, got a message that she was not at her desk, did not leave my name, said that I would call back. My obligation to myself not to forget is concluded.

The other L lived in relative tranquility for another week with her soon to be ex-husband. His almost endless capacity for abasement charmed her. He slept at the foot of the bed except on those occasions when it suited her to invite him under the covers.

He would make a noise to claim her attention and she would ask, "Who is it?" And he would announce himself as one of her lovers (she had a few months before confided her adulteries to him in novelistic detail), or present himself as some noted actor, or as a character out of a novel or film. If he chose someone she had in mind (or came reasonably close), she would hold out her hand to him. Sometimes she would hold out both arms.

One time when she asked him who he was he said, "Bela Lugosi. I've come to check out your precious fluids, my dear."

She was about to invite him to bed when the telephone interrupted them. A woman friend she hadn't seen in five years was on the phone, someone she could remember having missed. L invited her over, said to her missing friend, Natassia, that she had been about to embark on a liaison with Bela Lugosi when she called.

"I've had enough bloodsuckers in my life," said Natassia. When L got off the phone she asked her husband (calling him Bela) if he objected to having new blood around.

H, in one of his swaggering moods, said that he had no objection to entertaining both women. L said that she didn't know that that was in the cards but that she would give him his cue if and when the time came.

When Natassia arrived the two women embraced while the man of the house, costumed as a vampire, hung back in the shadows. L gushed at how unexpectedly terrific her friend looked, how radiant with health. "Don't you think so, Bela?" she asked her husband. They had been smoking dope awaiting Natassia's arrival. H, dressed in black cape, bowed formally, said in bogus eastern European accent, "To see the blood in your beautiful cheeks warms my heart."

What did Natassia, a no-nonsense, cerebral type, make of such behavior?

"Tell us what you've been doing with yourself," L said, passing around a joint. "We want to hear absolutely everything."

Natassia talked dispassionately of the recent dissolution of a love affair, a virtual marriage, that had lasted five years. The thing was, she said, she could feel nothing at all about the loss, or the man for that matter, neither regret nor exhil-

29

aration. In the past several months, she had become estranged from her feelings.

L said that sometimes people live with you for extended periods, and when they go you discover that they've taken up no real space in your life. They pass through your life like wisps of smoke. (She is ingesting smoke when she says this, so laughs self-consciously.) H twinkles at Natassia.

Natassia has more to say, though is not given the chance. "Isn't it marvelous to smoke again with old friends," said L with characteristic irrelevance.

"That is exactly what I wanted to say," said the serious Natassia, still musing apparently about the unaccountable muteness of her feelings.

They talked about going out for Chinese food but discarded the idea after making a meal of the discussion. Smoke becalmed appetite or increased it, did whatever you imagined it was doing.

The question came up. "Isn't Bela beautiful when he smokes?"

There was no way for Natassia to deny it without being rude, without abusing the rules of hospitality.

H brought a book into the room (an untranslated collection of Italian poems) and read to the women in a naive approximation of the language on the page.

Natassia made no sense of the words so assumed she was losing her mind. "He reads so nicely," she said to no one.

"When you don't know what the words mean," L said out of some pocket of memory, "you get much closer to the music of the language."

H continued to read aloud after the two women, by silent arrangement, had quit the living room. It was an aspect, L would have said, of an underrated integrity. H finished whatever he started no matter the inappropriateness of the context. He read for another fifteen minutes, with increasing stridency, to the empty room.

When the poems had run their course, H searched for the two women, found them in the master bedroom, asleep together, angled apart like an inverted 'v', on top of the lavendar-striped sheets of the queen-sized bed. It was not easy to know what to do next. He kissed his wife on the lips and heard her murmur another's unintelligible name, then he did the same to Natassia who put her arms around his neck. "I love you," he said to her.

"Don't say it, darling," Natassia said, putting her finger over his lips. "Don't say a word."

L woke to find her husband and friend in the first throes of the sexual act. Whatever else was happening, it was clear that penetration had been made. L had an extended moment of outrage to which she gave no voice. The least they could do, she thought, the very least, was to invite her to join them. She put her arms around them both, the position awkward and unpleasurable, though she was unable to wrest either's attention from the other.

I could understand what L was going through. Without prefiguration or warning, she had lost control of the world. The music she had been conducting so artfully had decided to take off on its own course, to conduct itself. A resourceful woman, L made a few phone calls to former lovers but could roust no one to take a fourth hand in the present game. I was one of the men she called, though I had never been her lover, had been merely someone she kept in mind for a rainy day or a dry month.

When she returned to the bedroom, Natassia and her husband were still making love, though at a retarded almost imperceptible pace. Their lethargy seemed positively comic, as if, literally, they were going through the motions. She wondered how to include herself, sat poised on her side of the bed, staring into space. "Why don't you join us?" one of them whispered, or perhaps she imagined the words in the rustle of breathing. A previously uncharted impulse gov-

31

erned her. Her affection for them both vanished like a fever, and she announced in a loud voice, "I want the two of you out of here. Immediately. Out of here."

No one protested. H and Natassia stopped what they were doing, dressed themselves with the same dreamy slow motion of their lovemaking, put on coats and hats, said goodbye to L, and left the apartment.

The next day, or perhaps even the same night, she called all her dearest friends to say that she had thrown her husband out and was now to be thought of as an unencumbered woman. To some others, usually the wives of former lovers, she simply said that H had moved out, said it in a choked voice to make it seem that she had been the mistreated one. She didn't know in truth who had mistreated whom, occupied herself with the sound of her voice telling the story of the last days of her marriage again and again to forestall an inevitable sense of loss.

So far, December has fewer cryptic notations than the preceding months. There has been no further mention of L, no exhortation to call for almost a month. *Buy gifts*, it says on December 10 and again on the 12th and 13th. Apparently to get anything done, I had to remind myself of the obligation more than once.

On Friday, 23 December: *Funeral, 10 A.M., Riverside Chapel.* It was not L's funeral, not L who had been married to H or the L I had been hesitant to call. It was the funeral of a former therapist who had died unexpectedly of a heart attack. He was an abrasive man, competitive, sometimes arrogant, always impatient with the least of my self-deceptions. Although I had never told him so, I felt indebted to him for whatever ability I had to move sanely in the world.

It makes me sad to see 1977 thin down to a few remaining leaves of calendar. I feel myself losing the year all over again, passing through it in accelerated time, rushing toward oblivion.

32

Who Shall Escape Whipping

On December 29, among a list of pre-New Year's resolutions, there it is again, number five in order of priority: *Call L.* Is it a new call, about some different matter, or has the advice to myself of two month's before been neglected this long? I regret the unconcluded call, rue it like some failure of character I can never hope to correct.

There are a number of discrepancies in the story of L's marriage to H. One of them stands out in particular. There is mention of a narrow bed belonging to a baby-sitter, but there are no babies in evidence in the story, no babies and no sitter.

At the funeral: friends of Kurt Mannheim were invited on stage to give personal testimony about the dead man. Two older men had already spoken at length when I felt compelled to get up. Despite my usual reticence—I've always distrusted exhibitionists, have held them in contempt—I went on stage as if I had something of unusual moment to say. Looking into the faces of the mourners, none of whom I really knew, I felt embarrassed and self-conscious. His wife, or a woman I assumed was his wife (I had never met her except in fantasy), was staring at me with what I took to be encouragement and sympathy. "I don't know why I'm up here," I started out saying. "I'm not, strictly speaking, a friend of Kurt's. I never saw him socially or met any of his family or friends, and to be honest, I was aggrieved with him more than half the period of our acquaintance. He once said to me—I can actually hear his voice at the moment— that I would never get up spontaneously before an audience because I had some stake in remaining aloof, that I was frightened to death of revealing myself as human (therefore mortal) like everyone else. He made that observation to me in the second year of what was to be a six-year therapy. Who the hell did he think he was to tell me that?" It was as if I were waiting for an answer. My throat constricted. Tears

33

pricked my eyes. When I could speak again, I mumbled the following, "I've gotten up here to make a fool of myself because it was something Kurt wanted me to be able to do. This . . . " I was unable to finish the sentence and have no recollection of getting off the stage and back to my seat. There was neither applause nor derision for my gesture (I had imagined applause), though Mrs. Mannheim came up to me after the ceremony and thanked me for my statement.

The sentence I didn't complete might have gone as follows: "This is to affirm, Kurt, that I am as mortal as you are." I don't know. I might have had something else in mind, something more appropriate and less self-concerned.

I remove the last two pages with some reluctance, pinch out the clips and insert the 1981 filler, giving me the illusion of having moved more than three years in the space of a few hours. So this is the present. It's nothing new.

When I get L on the phone she doesn't say, "Hello," but "Who is it?" as if accusing me of being an imposter. To protect myself, I give her a false name, say "This is Harold."

"Harold? Harold?" she says querulously in her hoarse voice. "Are you sure you have the right number? I don't know any Harolds outside of my father. You're not my father, are you?"

It strikes me that under a false name I am free to be more like myself. "Are you interested in going to a movie with me, Friday night?" I ask.

She gasps with what I take to be pleasurable surprise. "I'm dying to meet you, Harold," she says, "but I have this rule whereby I never go on dates with strange men."

I try to persuade her of my familiarity, but she is adamant about not violating her rule.

"Then there's no more to say," I say. (I knew it was a mistake to call, another occasion for humiliation.)

"Wait a sec, Harold," she says. "Don't go away, baby. I

just had this overwhelming perception that I know you from somewhere. Weren't we once an item? Weren't we once, under different names, an official couple? I have the idea that we have a lot of lost time to reclaim."

I didn't go away or hang up but in a moment or so we seemed to disconnect, a busy signal rising between us, then dead space. I would have called back, but I couldn't remember her number, couldn't find it listed in any of my address books.

I had lost her, I remember thinking in the dream, lost her without hope of recovery, emerging slowly from the bottom of some dark pool, waking open-mouthed, barely able to breathe, in an empty room in a silent house.

A FAMOUS

RUSSIAN

POET

A writer travels to a conference where he is to give a talk on other writers and participate on a panel discussing some issue of the day. He gives the talk, says only some of the things he intends, meets other writers, drinks with them. He goes to a reception for a famous Russian poet, who is the main guest of the conference. After that, he goes to a reading by the famous poet. There is another reception after the reading and the promise of several parties, but the writer avoids them all and goes to his motel room to sleep. The room is impersonal and unfamiliar. The writer is exhausted but unable to lose consciousness. He puts on the overhead light and writes for a few minutes in his notebook, describing briefly his experiences at the conference. Although he has had a lot to drink, he takes a Valium with a glass of water, worrying when it is done that he has endangered his life. Then he lies down on the bed with his hands under his head, thinking about what he has written. An hour passes. He considers that he is wasting time trying to sleep and gets up and walks about the room. The room is an odd configuration in the dark, is not as he remembered it in the light. He doesn't dare look at his watch, afraid of knowing how early it is, how much dead time he has still to get through. Why did he come to this conference? he asks himself. He turns on a lamp next to the television set, the ghostly light sliding along the wall. He leafs through the pages of a book of poems someone has given him, reading first and last lines, then turns off the lamp and goes back to sleep. His dreams are uneventful. There is not even the beginnings of a story in them.

He wakes up at 7:30, does some exercises (the same ones he does at home each morning), then takes a bath.

At ten after eight he goes out for breakfast, meets another visiting writer and they eat together. They talk about failed marriages and difficulties with children. They discover that they've had a number of similar experiences and decide to go for a walk in the country instead of returning to their rooms.

They pursue a country path in the general direction of the university at which the conference is being held, and find themselves temporarily lost. Their conversation is a continuation of what went before, is strewn with wives and children, with other writers, with friends they have in common. It is a beautiful day and they walk for a longer time than they had intended, each involved in his own elaborated past and how it is mirrored in the other's.

They return to the conference in the early afternoon for what is to be the main event of the second day, an Open Conversation with the famous Russian poet. The auditorium is filled and they are obliged to sit in the last row. The poet, who seems shy off the stage, has exceptional presence on, and even his most banal remarks are delivered with a solemnity and grace that enlivens them.

"The rest of us are here as spear carriers for him," the writer says to his companion.

His companion, he notices, has fallen asleep.

In answer to a question, the poet mentions that in Russia each of his books sells upwards of two hundred thousand copies.

Someone in the audience asks the Russian who his favorite American poets are.

The Russian poet hesitates before answering, though it is

a question, the writer imagines, he has answered many times before. He will answer the question, the celebrity says, by naming those poets whose work he feels is closest to his own oeuvre. Gary Snyder, he says, and of course Allen. The list extends itself, is as long as tact requires. The last name the famous poet mentions, the name brought up as an after-thought to his answer, is Bob Dylan.

Five years ago, the writer thinks, a student audience would have broken into applause at that point. This audience, heavy with respect, accepts the information as if it were its due.

After the interview with the famous poet is completed, the writer finds he has fifteen minutes to get ready for his own final performance. His mind, he discovers, is not on the subject of his panel but on whether they will have a car to get him to the airport after the panel is over.

He asks his companion, less joke than he makes it sound, if he knows what their subject is. His companion says he isn't sure, has lost his program, but that he thinks it's enti-tled, "The Esthetics of the New Fiction," or something to that effect.

The writer imagines the three panelists sitting on the stage, offering the audience an hour of silence.

The writer goes up on the stage with the others, trusting his remarks to chance. The third panelist, also without a program, has a wholly different idea of the topic, has come prepared to talk about the process of his own writing.

They are asked by the Assistant Director of the Confer-ence not to start until some more people arrive. There are only two people in the audience as they sit down on the stage. One is reading a student newspaper; the other, after staring nervously about the empty auditorium, closes her eyes.

The panelists decide to wait another ten minutes before beginning, discussing procedure in whispers among themselves, the live microphone on the table picking some of it up and broadcasting it to the small audience. The writer, it is agreed, will make his statement last.

Two more people come in, seat themselves in the back row close to the aisle. Another straggler follows, looks embarrassed and turns and leaves. The woman who has closed her eyes begins to snore, attracting amused notice.

Fifteen minutes pass. Audience and panel exchange shy glances. The writer looks at his watch. He has to be at the airport in an hour and ten minutes to make his flight.

Gradually, the discussion starts. Since there is no clear subject at issue, the subject becomes the panelists themselves. The small audience—there are now seven in all—listen in with the anxiety (or so it seems to the writer) of being trapped in a place they don't want to be. Their faces remind him of pictures he's seen of prisoners of war.

When it is the writer's turn to speak, he finds himself unable to begin.

"I am a Jew," he says after a while as a means of introducing himself, a remark he had no intention of making and which embarrasses him to hear, "though not conventionally religious. I am most aware of being Jewish in places where everyone else is not. In the army, for example," (he has not been in the army for twenty years) "I went to services every Friday night except when the opportunity was denied me. To know that is essential to an understanding of my work.

"I have been married three times, though am not at the present. That is to say, I am separated from my third wife. I have difficulty living alone—perhaps this is a universal paradox—though cherish privacy, indeed need it in order to write. I have had three children, one by each of my wives. Their ages are twelve, nine and four. None lives with me, though the twelve-year-old, Arthur, did at one time. Visiting with them is an ordeal for me, particularly with the youngest. I identify with him, I think, suffer the pangs of

39

separation when I return him to his mother. It's as if my father were leaving me. I don't mind living alone, have come to appreciate the freedom it offers, though since the break-up of my most recent marriage, I have had three different women stay with me for short periods of time. What I am looking for eludes me. I am a monogamous man, or like to think of myself as such. I haven't had an extramarital affair that hasn't left me with grief and feelings of guilt."

Why am I going on like this? he asks himself. The faces around him, in the audience and on the stage, provide no answer.

"I don't mean to expose myself to you this way," he says, "but this is the only subject on which I have pretensions to expertise." (Wait for the laugh, he tells himself, aware that he is a performer on a stage.) "When you are away from home and have nothing specific to do, you think about your life. Perhaps *you* don't and I do. All morning I talked about my life to a friend I hardly know. I am in the mood to continue if you are in the mood to listen. The esthetic of my work is to write what it pleases me to write. I can't explain that in philosophic terms—I never think of it abstractly—but I can exemplify it for you in my performance. All right?"

The writer stops again and looks around the mostly naked auditorium. There is sympathy, he thinks, in the eyes of at least one of his eavesdroppers. That sympathy—perhaps it is only that she is thinking of something moving in her own life—impells him to continue.

"Despite the apparent evidence against it, I am a monogamous man and a domestic one. I like comfort and elegance—I drive an old Mercedes sedan prohibitively expensive to maintain—and can think of nothing more desirable than to be surrounded by wife, children and intimate friends. Yet, at this juncture of my life, at the age of forty-four, I am living alone and valuing the benefits of that solitude. All right? My most recent wife, Felice, left me because

I was sleeping with other women, though she didn't actually move out until six months after that part of my life was over. That's what makes me angry—both sad and angry—that she waited until I had committed myself unequivocally to our marriage then left me for someone else. Had she stayed, I believe I would have remained faithful to her for as long as we were together. I think it took me five years of marriage to fall in love with her. That's an odd thing to say, isn't it? We never should have gotten married in the first place. I met Felice at a writer's conference similar to this one. I was married at the time to Helena, my second, though that was already on the rocks. Felice had the motel room two doors down from mine. I couldn't sleep and went out for a walk at three in the morning. Her light was on. She was reading a book. What do the circumstances matter? The book she was reading was one of mine. How could I resist that omen? Although outside her door, I was already in her hands.

"In about fifteen minutes there is supposed to be a car outside to take me to the airport, so I don't want to get carried away. I am hoping, it is my method in all things, to bring this statement to a conclusive point, to discover its point, and leave some time for my colleagues to make whatever further comments they have in store. Bear with me. I think there is an intelligible core to my ramblings, an informing idea, as critics like to say. I am neither drunk nor insane, at least not so insane as to have it an issue between us. You have come to this conference—I am talking also to those who are not here—to see———, who is a famous poet. Justly famous. A visitor from a far planet. The rest of us are here to fill out the conference with peripheral activity. We are the curtain raisers and anticlimaxes surrounding the main event. When I sit down to write in my apartment, denuded of wives and children, denuded of life-filling distractions, I am the main event myself. I miss that momentarily, regret the loss of my own centrality. For that reason, perhaps for others I don't understand, instead of talking about esthetics, which I never think of in connection with my own work, I told you something about my life, about its peculiar though undistinctive disarray. While I am telling you about this serious comedy, my life, I am reimagining it as a fiction, I am. . . . "

His friend next to him nudges him with an elbow, which is fortunate since he is caught in his last sentence without hope of extrication. "It's time for you to leave for the airport," he says.

The writer, in a state of exhilaration, excuses himself and gets down from the podium. The woman, who was asleep, wakes herself to applaud.

When he gets outside the auditorium, there is no car waiting for him, though it is already five minutes past the appointed time. The writer, in a state of panic, locates the Assistant Director of the Conference and is told the university car has gone to get the Russian poet, and unless there is a further misunderstanding will come back for the writer in a few minutes.

So he sits on the steps of the building, waiting, his exhilaration metamorphosing into depression, checking his watch from time to time. He assumes that he has been forgotten, that the car will not show up, though continues to wait out of inertia, his imagination failing him in regard to other choices.

Finally, the car arrives. The Russian poet, impassive as ever, is in the front seat next to the driver. The writer is introduced to the famous poet. The Russian, he can tell, has never heard of him. The writer sits in the back seat next to the poet's luggage. Unless his watch is misinformed, they have twenty minutes to get to the airport. He is surprised that no one else is concerned with the shortness of time.

They arrive at the airport four minutes before the plane's

scheduled departure. The driver, who is also one of the organizers of the conference, carries the famous poet's luggage, while the writer carries his own, an overnight bag and a briefcase filled mostly with his own books.

The writer sits next to the famous poet on the flight and they make a few awkward attempts at conversation.

The writer asks the famous poet how much longer he'll be in America.

The poet says that he'll be on tour for three more weeks.

The writer asks the poet how old he is and the poet, noticeably surprised at the question, says he is forty-two.

The writer asks the poet if he finds it wearing to move from university to university, never staying at any one place long enough to have any real sense of what it's like.

The poet says, no, he is used to it, that it is all right. The travel is not . . . against his pleasure.

The writer, though aware he is talking about something else, says he gets no pleasure from such trips himself and usually avoids them.

The writer becomes self-consciously aware of the banality of his conversation, would like to say something of larger import to the poet, though doesn't know where to begin.

"What do you write?" the poet asks him, turning from the window to inquire.

Although the poet's enunciation tends to be precise, the writer misunderstands the question and proceeds to justify his practice as a writer in the face of a small, vaguely comprehending audience. He can hear himself go on too long.

"I asked *what* you write," says the poet sternly.

"Fiction," says the writer, "mostly short stories. There are two novels." He thinks of giving the famous poet one of his books, though is embarrassed to make the gesture.

"I like American novels," says the famous poet. "I like U——"[a celebrated novelist] "whom I met in Leningrad and again in Boston. Do you know him?"

43

"I've met him once," says the writer. "To be frank, I don't really like his work."

"It is sexy," says the famous poet, smiling and turning to the window. "That is what I like about it that it is sexy."

They complete the flight to La Guardia without further conversation. The writer imagines a further exchange between them in the extended silence. He writes their unspoken dialogue down in the notebook he keeps in the breast pocket of his jacket.

Someone from the Russian embassy awaits the poet. The writer nods good-bye, avoiding the awkward excess of a further gesture, then takes a cab back to his apartment in the West 20's. Before taking off his jacket, before making himself a drink, he visits each of his five rooms. The apartment is the way the writer left it the morning before to go to the airport, familiar and bereft, the debris in its own reasonable order, the rooms conspicuously empty of other life. He hangs up his jacket in the foyer closet, sits down at the desk in his study and in longhand on a legal-sized sheet of yellow paper begins a story. It starts well, he thinks, admiring the rhythm of his opening paragraph, but what will happen to it along the way? He imagines the Russian poet reading over his shoulder. There will be no sex in it, none or very little. The story goes on as he wants it, resists all pressure to make it other than it is.

HOW YOU

PLAY THE

GAME

"You ought to write a story about basketball," my wife said to me in bed one evening. We had been on the West Coast for two weeks, and I hadn't written a sentence that had survived a second reading. "You spend so much time watching basketball and obsessing about it, the least you can do is transform it into art."

"It's already art," I said.

Genevieve kicked me in the leg with characteristic overstatement. "That's an evasive remark and *you* know it. It's not literary art, is it? I've heard you say that all subjects are susceptible to imaginative transformation."

I had no recollection of the remark and said so.

After a prolonged silence, time passing like a bird flying through a room, she whispered, "Joshua, are you awake? . . . You could write a story about a man who obsessively identifies with a losing team, who is paranoid about officials, who can't get to sleep after a game and carries the defeats of his team around with him as if they were personal failures."

"What you're describing is a situation not a narrative," I said.

"You don't expect me to do the whole story for you, do you? Imagine some of it for yourself."

Although I prodded it, the imagination didn't move.

The discussion resumed over breakfast; that is Genevieve, who is something of an obsessive herself, reopened the subject. "Do you have any ideas for the story?" she asked.

I hadn't, but I said I had.

"Do you want to talk about them?" she asked in the tone of a former therapist.

I improvised. "The main character replays losing games in his mind, altering the results, ultimately confusing the real game with his invented game."

"I don't like it," she said, disappearing temporarily into the underbrush of the kitchen.

We talked about the weather after that, and I recounted the shards of a half-remembered dream.

The basketball story, as Genevieve refers to it, occupies me like an obligation. Perhaps if I can locate an opening sentence, the story will proceed apace. No beginnings offer themselves.

At the heart of the story is the fan's obsession. On the day of a televised game he works himself into emotional readiness by playing out a range of scenarios in his head, anticipating the best and worst to avoid both surprise and disappointment. He invites sympathetic presences to spectate with him, but it is rare that anyone comes. His reputation as a fanatic has become so extensive that even those who don't know him well decline his invitation. The game is his alone, an unshared responsibility. Sometimes he forces his wife to sit next to him, ties her to the seat.

I am unable to decide whether to use real teams or invented teams in the story.

"I don't see that it makes any difference," my wife says dogmatically. She suggests presenting the question to our recent friends, the Blooms, when they come by for a drink.

The Blooms seem happy to discuss the problem with us,

though their choices cancel out one another and become the occasion of a fight between them.

"Of course you have to use real team names," Viola says. "I think you know that, though you want to have someone else verify it for you."

"It's a fiction," Henry says. "It's an imagined world we're talking about. Don't be so absolute."

"Who's being absolute, Henry, you or me? You're the one that's being absolute. What do you think, Genevieve?"

Genevieve refills their glasses with Inglenook Colombard, a nice little wine of no distinction. "I don't think it matters. I think the question is academic."

Viola reiterates her position with even more certitude than before. Henry shouts, "Nonsense." I suggest a changing of the subject, but the subject won't go away.

The next morning, putting everything else aside, I write out some notes for the basketball story.

Opens with a dream in which the dreamer has been made coach of a basketball team and decides at the last moment to suit up as one of the players. The dream ends with him standing at the foul line waiting to take a shot that could tie the game.

A possible compromise: to use the names of real teams, but to invent the names of the ballplayers—perhaps instead of names to use numbers. 6 takes a bounce pass from 14, moves behind a pick set by 21, and hits an eighteen-foot jump shot.

There are sixteen seconds to go. The central character is listening to a tape of a game that his team had lost in the last minute, involved in the action as if the outcome were still open to negotiation.

"Interesting," Genevieve says. "What do the people who live with him think of his behavior?"

47

"I don't know. How do you think they'd react?"

Genevieve walks away without a word or, as is sometimes the case, thinking she's answered when she hasn't, her answer spoken silently or sulkingly encoded in gesture.

There are fifteen seconds to go. The opposing team, down by one, has the ball out at midcourt. A time out has been called. The television breaks for a series of commercials while the teams plan strategies.

The observer nurses a brandy, his chest tight, hands tingling. Will they remember to box out after the shot? he worries.

The phone rings inopportunely. "Son of a bitch," he shouts. "Tell whoever it is I'll call back later."

The game returns to the nineteen-inch screen.

Not enough pressure on the inbounds pass, he thinks, inuring himself to defeat.

"The Blooms want us to go to the coast with them on Sunday," his wife says. "What should I tell them?"

One of their guards is killing time, dribbling in place, working the clock to eight seconds before making his move toward the basket. Perhaps the play is set up for him to pass underneath.

"Well, do you want to go or not?"

Fairchild dribbles to the left, to the right, edging closer to the basket with each turn. Number 12 on the Knicks defenses him. Fairchild fakes twice, trying to pick up a foul, before getting off a forced shot with five seconds on the clock. The ball hits the back of the rim and rises above the basket, rises, floats. The seconds are down to three, the neon numbers flickering, changing shape as they decline.

A hand goes up, hesitates, comes down. The ball is tipped, skitters off the rim. One second left. The ball is tipped again, hits off the backboard, rims the basket seductively, then falls to the side as the buzzer sounds.

"If you want to go, it's all right with me."
We win by one. The final score . . .

The tip goes in as the buzzer sounds, and I shut off the set in a rage of frustration. It seemed to be slipping off until it reversed itself, caught the inside of the rim and dropped.

One of the guards on the Hawks is working the clock, moving the ball with magical fingers against the hard wood. He puts the ball behind his back, comes out empty-handed. 12 on the Knicks has stolen the ball, is driving downcourt with gratuitous urgency as the clock ticks away. He is cut off at the foul line, so dribbles off to the side where someone grabs his arm, forcing the ball loose and out of bounds. There is no foul call. Ball goes over to the Hawks with five seconds left in the game. 12's fury is nothing to my own. We both shout at the official, turn our faces away in disdain. "How could he lose the ball without being fouled? I ask, barely raising my voice, but a commercial for deodorant intervenes.

There are four seconds on the clock. Genevieve comes into the room to ask if the game is over, watches Fairchild of the Hawks throw a high looping pass under the basket. One of our players knocks it away, but it falls circumstantially into the hands of one of their guards at the foul line. There should be almost no time left. A desperation shot goes up amid a flurry of waving arms. "Shh," I say to my wife. "Don't move." She is already out of the room, walking away. The shot falls short. The buzzer sounds while it is still hopelessly in flight. "We won it," I call out, but my exhilaration is premature. The players are crowding around the officials, awaiting some decision. The announcer informs us that the shooter has been fouled in the act of shooting and will have two free throws. If he makes them both, the

49

Hawks will win by one point. I turn off the set, unable to watch the inevitable conclusion.

She is huddling in a corner of the living room when I come in, a book in front of her face. I grumble something, clear my throat of exasperation. "I don't want to hear about it," she says. "Why do you let yourself get so upset? I can't stand to listen to you watch."
"Who tells you to listen?"
"Who tells you to watch?"
It is the same exchange we've had before, a slow-motion replay of former conversation.

She asks him: "Is it worse when you lose or worse when you win?" The tension afterward, he would tell her, tends to be worse when his team wins. Losing is, after all, a kind of release. Winning invites retribution, generates anxiety and a certain amount of guilt. Still, his commitment as a fan is to winning at any cost.
He defers answer to her question.

The fearsome Lakers are ahead by fourteen points with six minutes left on the clock, the game apparently irretrievable. The central character of my story watches with a scholar's distance. The Knicks hit two unanswered baskets in quick succession, and the possibility of heroic reversal tempts him, despite himself, to hope. He turns off the set and pours himself a glass of red wine, an inexpensive Valpocella of negligible ambition. After two or three sips, his calm tentatively restored, he pushes the button that brings the game back to life. At the very moment, the fan and the game engage one another, the Knicks score on a fast break, which cuts the Laker lead to ten with barely over three minutes to go. There has been no progress in his absence. He resigns himself to defeat. The Knicks hit on the next three baskets, two on sleight-of-hand steals, and have suddenly closed the gap to four. Anything is possible. The fan can no longer sit in his chair, walks into the kitchen for a second glass of wine, though he can barely remember having entertained the first.

The Knicks are one point down with a minute and eight seconds to play. The fan stands up to stretch, can barely lift his arms. The Lakers score on a tip-in of a missed shot, and the lead is stretched to three. Chances are slim, the character thinks, if not absolutely hopeless. The Knicks come down in a hurry and lose the ball on an errant pass. "Stupid," he complains, taking the blame on himself, hopes dashed. The Lakers run the clock down to twenty seconds before forcing a shot in a crowd. 18 takes the rebound and throws a full court pass to 12 who scores on a driving lay-up (the fan thinks he was also fouled, but no call is made), cutting the lead to one point with twelve seconds to go. The Lakers call time out, and the television cuts away to a beer commercial. The fan refuses hope, yet triumphant scenarios embrace the imagination unbidden. The Knicks pick off the inbounds pass, or the Lakers are unable to get the ball into play in the allotted five seconds and so lose possession. The Knicks design a play in which 18 will end up with the shot behind a double screen. The shot is released from the right corner with five seconds left and hangs in the air for an unconscionable time. The fan, guiding the ball invisibly, can't bring himself to let it drop in the basket.

Triumphant scenarios embrace the imagination unbidden. 12 gets the ball on an inbounds pass and goes down the middle, inviting a foul from the opposition. He scores on an underhand lay-up and the Laker lead is cut to one with ten seconds to go. The Lakers call time out, and the television cuts away to a shaving commercial for a razor with a pivotal

51

head. The fan paces the room, hopeful, yet refusing hope. The Lakers, emerging from the commercial, get the ball in to their brilliant center, who is also the tallest man in the game. 12 slaps the ball loose from the blind side and streaks down the court. Two Laker players converge on him. 12 throws the ball behind his back to number 21, who takes a short jump shot and misses, the rebound tricking into one of the Lakers' hands. Time runs out. The Knicks lose by one.

"Is the story going to interest anyone that doesn't follow basketball," Genevieve asks. "The language is like a code, don't you think?"

"I'm thinking of discarding the story," I say.

The news embitters her, creates a wall of silence between us. In bed, her back to me, I plead for an explanation, rue the error of my ways.

It takes a while to penetrate her silence. A day or two passes. "You refuse to write the story," she whispers one evening, "because I was the one that suggested it. You make me responsible for your failure."

Number 18 scissors down the lane, pulls up abruptly, jumps, releases the ball barely over the extension of the defender. The ball fills the hole as the buzzer goes off. "It's good," the announcer screams, validating my vision of it. The game is over. The Knicks win by one. I am unable to get out of my chair.

I wake at 2 A.M., exhausted from running up and down the court, my heart racing. I lie stiffly on my back, courting sleep. Free underneath, I hold up my hands, call for the ball. Whoever has it—it looks like my kid brother Alex—takes a bad shot rather than pass it to the open man. No sense of the game, these kids. I pick off the rebound, knocking someone out of my way. "I can't go back to sleep," I say to Genevieve as she turns my way, hooking a leg around mine. She opens her eyes, says not a word. I shoot out of the corner and make the shot.

Fouled on the shot (why else would I miss?), I go to the line, study the basket, bounce the ball eight times as I had seen others do and . . .

"I noticed the story in your typewriter," she mentions over breakfast, "and I think using numbers instead of names is a mistake."

"You think I ought to use the names of real players?"

"Maybe." She kisses me in passing, puts an arm around my waist. "I'm glad you haven't given up the story. I think it's nice that you go at something that's difficult for you to resolve."

Before I go to sleep each night, I shoot five imaginary foul shots. It's not a good night unless I make four out of five.

There are nine seconds left in the second overtime. We are ahead by two and in possession of the ball. The coach has brought me in to make the inbounds pass, relying on my sense of the appropriate. No one is free to receive the ball, the opposing players attaching themselves to my teammates like sets of Siamese twins. I throw the ball high in the air toward our basket, hoping to use up the clock. Players from both teams converge toward the ball. Someone hits it back into the air like a balloon, and the clock ticks off the seconds as it rises and descends. The Trail Blazers recover the ball with five seconds to go—a slow clock it seems to me—and move abruptly toward the other end, passing the ball among them as they go. "What have you done?" the coach yells from the bench. "You've courted disaster."

53

There is something too conclusive in winning, he thinks.
It leaves no room for regret.

"Why don't you root for a winning team sometimes?" she
asks in response to one of my periodic complaints about my
team's failure to live up to expectations.
"I would," I say, "if the team I rooted for won."

The main character of my story turns the set off at half-
time with his team behind by fifteen. He asks his wife if
she'd like to make love, kissing her ear first to show the
manifest seriousness of his intentions. She smiles slyly, says I
hadn't thought of it until you asked. Heh heh. They undress
in the dark, exchange hands, slide like fish under the covers.
There are five minutes to play in the third quarter, he
thinks, catching the numbers on the digital clock just before
he enters her. He thinks of himself as Number 12 driving
through the key, eluding two defenders (he kisses her breasts,
moving from one to another out of sense of fair play), pene-
trating to the basket for the score. He falls asleep with his
wife across his chest like a banner, then wakes abruptly.
The game is almost over, something tells him. He slips out
of his wife's arms and out of the bed and down the stairs to
the television set. Expectancy tenses him. He tries to deter-
mine the situation from the sound of the crowd. The extended cheering is ominous. The score is tied at 100, the announcer informs him, with two minutes and five seconds to
play. The Bullets, the home team, have just scored the tying
goal which explains the applause of the crowd.

What is hard for him is to write about the game in fiction
while being obsessive about real games in real life. His losses
are too immediate, too painful, though being on the West
Coast provides a certain metaphorical distance. Josh
mentions his conflict to a friend, who advises him to put the

story aside. "I can't," he says, "Genevieve will be heartbroken. And besides the story has gone too far in the manifest world to return to the state of unadulterated idea."

I talk to them during the time out, suggest the playing of defense as a useful corrective. "What's corrective mean exactly?" Number 12 asks. "I know the etymology of the word defense. The word corrective isn't in my lexicon."

"Make them know they have an opponent," I say. "Put your bodies on the line."

"You mean on the foul line?" Number 3 asks. "Man, some dude has gots to foul you first." He looks at me as if I had left my senses in the locker room.

"What I'm saying is, I want you guys to block up the middle and not let those thugs in the red and white uniforms get unmolested shots."

"We'll molest them for you, coach," they say.

They go out and play defense like madmen, guarding all over the floor. It makes no difference. The other team, the Bulls, continue to score.

The Bulls are a man short and I am asked to play with them against my own team to even the sides. The uniform they have for me is a bit tight in the crotch and I ask the trainer for something in a larger size. The second uniform I'm issued is larger than the first was small, the shorts extending significantly beyond the knees. I think of it as a form of disguise. It amuses my teammates and creates a sense of esprit on a team reputed to be in disarray. When I miss a shot underneath early in the game my new teammates begin to distrust my intentions. After that I don't see the ball again, though I'm often free for a shot, standing alone under the basket like an orphan. I have to intercept passes from my teammates just to get into the game. We, the we I'm playing with, are two points down. The other we, my real team (the team I bleed for), are two points ahead. I hit a one-handed pop shot from the side and tie the score. "I thought you were one of us," Number 12 says as he passes. "You can't have it both ways."

As I move downcourt to play defense, one of my circumstantial teammates asks me what number 12 had said. I shrug, refuse betrayal, indicate that it was of no importance.

In the second half—the switching of baskets is responsible—I have trouble recalling which of the teams I am playing against and which for, aware only that it is the opposite of what one might expect. I recall that I am playing against my real team, but have lost track which of the two teams that is—the team whose uniform I'm wearing or the team whose uniform I once wore. Both teams at this point are equally familiar and equally unsympathetic. The team, wearing my uniform, has been ahead much of the game by four or two points. A hook shot by Number 12, cutting across the circle, cuts the margin to two. Abruptly the ball comes to me, a pass or interception. Players on both teams make appeal for its return. I drive for the furthest basket and in a confusion of bodies, score the tying basket. "You shot the wrong hoop, man," one of my teammates whispers to me. I hold up my arms to acknowledge the cheers.

"You haven't watched a game all week," my wife observes. "Is the season over?"

"We're on the West Coast," I remind her. "Besides the real game gets in the way of the fiction."

That gives her a laugh, which is nice, since she is not easily entertained. "Well, my love, if it takes you long enough to write this story, you'll cure yourself of being a fan."

Is it one of those occasions, I wonder, where the cure is more pernicious than the disease?

The coach is ejected from the game for unseemly behavior, and I am unexpectedly put in charge of the team. We are losing by seventeen, so that there is not much in the way of coaching required, which is just as well because I can't remember a single play. I call a time out to introduce myself to my charges, to clarify the change of command. I have nothing to say to them in the huddle, no adjustments to make, no advice or strategy to offer. "Keep coming at them," I say, waving my fist in the air. They nod to a man and return to the playing surface in an inspirited manner. In three minutes the lead is reduced to nine. The Spurs call time out. Again I am silent in the huddle, withhold the few banalities that hurriedly come to mind, waiting for the *mot juste*. "Keep it up," I yell after them as they return to the floor. They continue as before, playing unimaginably well, and reduce the lead to three. The lead moves between three and five—my team looks tired suddenly—in the next few minutes and the player seated next to me, Bartleby, asks if he can go in to give Number 12 a blow. "I don't like to remove a winning combination," I say, though don't know that he's not right. When the lead extends itself again to five, I send in three substitutes. The players returning to the bench complain about being replaced. "Do you want to win the game, coach, or are you in the pay of a foreign power?" 12 says to me as he takes his place on the bench. "Aren't you tired?" I ask him. "Man, I'm always tired," he says. "There's no percentage not being tired." The game goes badly in the short run and I panic and send back the regulars. They reduce the lead to two with a minute to go, but there is something in their play, something almost imperceptible, that forebodes defeat. They have in the next thirty seconds three separate occasions to tie the score. Each time the ball refuses to go in, skimming or rimming the basket. It suggests to me a failure of intent. The other team seems equally conflicted; each time they get the ball, they tend to make a careless mistake and give it back. But it's no use—we can't score or won't. They come off the court at the game's end, heads down in dismay, unable to hide their feelings of humiliation. "You didn't really try," I say, unable to hold it back. "They were asking to be beaten." "Come on, coach," says 12, "we did just what you wanted us to do. This bunch of gents aims to please."

Williams brings the ball up court in a hurry, passes it into Russell at the high post, slips underneath the basket, takes a return pass, and puts the ball in over his shoulder. He is fouled but no foul is called. We win 115 to 114.

"Does that make you happy?" she asks.

"Does that make you happy?" Genevieve asks. We are in bed and the occasion of her remark is fraught with ambiguity. We are lying on our sides facing each other, kissing openmouthed. It is a day of travel. The team is on the road somewhere between Denver and Seattle, perhaps boarding a plane at this very moment. The hero of my story moves with them through the crowd of spectators, keeping up morale by a stream of chatter. "Take it to them," he chants. "You're looking good. Keep it up. Make 'em sorry. We're number one."

As he enters his wife, he hears the roar of the crowd. The jumbo jet is lifting off the runway, ascending to the stratosphere without him. A game between unknown players is being played on the radio next door. It is, no doubt, a West Coast game. He hears cheering, an extended applause. "Does that make you happy, Joshua?" she asks. The answer is implicit, though unacknowledged even to himself, is somewhere in the room with them. "I'm as happy as I ever am," he says, a harmless lie. What happens next takes his breath away.

In the final seconds, we lose by one.

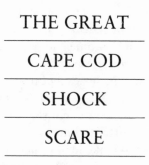

THE GREAT

CAPE COD

SHOCK

SCARE

One day a man swimming off the point returned to shore with much, if not most, of his leg missing. He was as surprised as the rest of us to discover what had happened.

The incident put a damper on our vacation. It was as if an alien force, boding no good, had entered our world.

We continued our summer routine, continued to do the things we had been doing, as if to admit the reality of this intrusion was to give up everything.

Some of the summer people kept their children out of the water for a week or so after the incident, though most of us felt that what had happened to the man (the loss of half of his left leg) was a singular occurrence and of little consequence to the rest of us.

(Little did we know.)

Not five days after the man (a stranger to most of us) had lost his leg in the water, Alfie Knopf (12), who was a strong swimmer for his size, emerged from a dive into the waves with his head torn off.

This was different. Alfie Knopf was known, more or less, to all of us. He played the outfield in our weekly softball games. Whatever had killed poor Alfie in such a pitiless manner could not be countenanced indefinitely.

59

This was the beginning—the early volleys so to speak—of what has been called *The Great Cape Cod Bicentennial Shock Scare*. No shock at that time had been sighted, but we all assumed that that's what it was.

All of us assumed the obvious except my wife Genevieve, who put it down to providence. "There's something there that doesn't want us in the water," she would say, only partly (one half to one fourth) kidding.

The rest of us tended to make light of her portentousness, and she took a lot of teasing that summer from our friends. Time would vindicate her. She had a history of being vindicated by time.

A side effect of the crisis was a run on books in the local libraries dealing with ocean predators. We were hungry to know what the adversary did in his spare time, what his habits were and habitat, his *modus vivendi*. There were not enough books on shocks to go around so some of us became experts on stingrays, piranhas and poisonous underwater plants.

It was mostly unspoken, though clearly it was on everyone's mind: When would the killer of the sea strike again?

We didn't, as it turned out, have long to wait.

An old man named Perez, casting for his dinner in a rickety fishing boat, became the dinner of someone or something else. He was a brave old man, who had once seen Joe DiMaggio play centerfield for the Yankees, though had been fishing out of his depths. We learned from this incident that being in a boat was no guarantor of safe passage.

A few days after that—it was on August 1, as I remember—the first shock hunting party set out. On August 5, an empty boat returned.

The hunt was our main topic of conversation when we got together over cocktails each evening. Rumors and fantasies passed among us, enlivened by irony and the postures of sophistication.

My friend Ugo had fantasies of taking on the shock single-handedly, *mano a mano*, and talked for days of little else.

The cocktail parties were particularly hard on the women who tended to be bored by all the shock talk. "I've had it," Genevieve announced one night after leaving the Lipman's. "No one talks about books or movies or whose marriage is breaking up anymore. If you want to go to those parties, you'll have to go without me."

I told her that I didn't enjoy the parties any more than she did, and added that the shock talk was merely fad and would pass in time.

"If it wasn't the shock, it would be some other unnatural disaster," she said. "The shock fulfills a real need for this community. I'm surprised you don't see that. It gives it a center of focus without which it cannot do."

I tended to think that everything was both true and false that summer so I didn't argue the point with her. Meanwhile the mutilations and deaths were piling up in unobtrusive profusion. The shock, if that's what it was (no one had seen it or too many had seen it in too many different places), could be ignored only at our peril.

The second hunting party spent six days and five nights without making contact with the predator. No one knew quite what to make of it. The shock, it seemed, had a predilection for the defenseless.

It touched us and it didn't. Although we followed the exploits of shock and shock-hunter with a certain fascination, the actual events seemed remote from our lives like a film we had seen on television and forgotten the next day.

Genevieve in bed one night: "Your shock is pressing up against my thigh."

So it was that the predator insinuated itself into our daily vocabulary.

Our neighbor, Anna, joking about her children, would say, "I wonder where my little predators are."

Little jokes covered over unspoken, perhaps unspeakable terrors.

We could only guess at what was going on in the mind of the shock, though there was no paucity of theories. He hated the human race, a visiting psychologist posited, for its presumptive superiority to his own.

Anna's husband, Ugo, had a dream in which he captured and killed the shock, stabbing the sea monster repeatedly in the tail with a fish-cleaning knife.

The dream, as it might, fired Ugo's imagination. He read it as an omen, a strategy from the unconscious. "The trick is," he said over drinks at our house that night, "is to take him from behind. If you stay away from his teeth, he can't do any great damage to you."

Genevieve had her hands over her ears.

"In this dream, I held the sonofabitch around the tail, my knife between my teeth, and he thrashed about in the water, trying to shake me loose. He couldn't do it. No matter what he did, I held fast, my hands coated with a stickum substance that professional footballers use. He couldn't understand why he couldn't free himself of me and eventually, you could tell, it broke his spirit. Then—the timing had to be perfect or I was dead—I went for the kill."

Throughout the recounting of this dream, Anna had this big sly smile on her face. We all knew, though never talked about it directly, that their marriage was in trouble.

"The shock has put Ugo in a very macho mood," said Anna.

The next day at The Grand Union, while we were checking out the groceries, Ugo suggested with a wink that we go out together in his cabin cruiser tomorrow and do some deep-water fishing.

I didn't mind, I said, but it would have to be after lunch as I used the mornings to write.

If what I said registered, there was no indication of it on Ugo's face. "We'll need a crew of four," he was saying. "What do you think? I'd like to get Norman and Ron or Hennessey and Eastlake. Do you see what I'm aiming at? The right combination of chemistries, a self-generating tension."

There was something solid about Ugo beneath the quirkiness. If I was going to risk my life in some quixotic pursuit, there was no one among our acquaintances I would rather have on my side.

We didn't set out the next day or the next one either, although we had an understanding, Ugo and I. We talked about it as our impending deep-sea fishing expedition.

On a Friday, twelve perhaps thirteen days after the first shock incident, we received a verifiable sighting of the predator. He had been seen ten miles off the coast of North Truro, cavorting in the waves with what appeared to be a human hand in his mouth. The hand to this day remains unidentified, one of the continuing mysteries of the whole affair.

On Saturday at 10 A.M., we started out on our expedition. There were four of us, Ugo, myself, Hank Quixote, and a fat southern Irishman named Forster Hennessey. "With a crew like that," said Genevieve, who had been against my going, "you don't have to look outside the boat for an enemy."

She might have said the same thing about any four or five of us that summer, but as it turned out she was more than usually right. While Hank, who is an inveterate complainer and intellectual, seems to enjoy physical labor—some compensatory principle operating there—Forster Hennessey, a mountainous man given to sloth and fat, generally does as little work as the traffic will bear, preferring talk and drink and the violence of metaphor.

We were a mile or two off shore, Hennessey on his fourth

ale and in the middle of what seemed like an endless mono-
logue, when Ugo called us all together to assert his authority.

"There can be only one captain on a ship," he started out.
"I'd like to get that out of the way so that there'll be no
misunderstanding later on. I served in the Navy in the last
war, so I know what I'm talking about when I say that our
survival may depend on how decisively the captain gives
orders and how quickly the crew responds to them."

Hennessey belched again. "Come off it Ugo," he said. "If
you want to be captain, you can be captain. It's your boat,
man. Just don't be so heavy about it, huh?"

Ugo transformed himself before our eyes into some self-
created image of captaincy, puffing out his cheeks like
Charles Laughton as he informed us of our duties. I was to
be second in command, or first mate as he called it, to
become captain if the original were in some manner incapa-
citated. (I would have declined if given the choice—but no
choice was forthcoming.) Quixote and Hennessey were to
share, no status distinction between them, the remaining
chores of crew. Ugo would treat us as men, he said, so long
as we behaved as men. He wore a pistol and walked up and
down the deck, as he delivered himself of the terms of his
command. If I hadn't known him as well as I had, I would
have thought that he had taken leave of his senses, had
moved beyond the pale of eccentricity into outright mad-
ness.

Before he dismissed us, Ugo produced a pint bottle of
blood—for a moment I thought he was going to ask us to
drink from it—which was to be the bait to lure the shock
from its depths. "It is my blood," he said, "and it will do
what is expected of it."

The next morning Hennessey was ordered to paint a thick
stripe of blood on the right side of the boat, an order he
accepted to our surprise without even an obligatory display
of resistance.

"What if the shock finds Ugo's blood unappetizing?" Hennessey asked me later just loud enough for the captain to hear.

"Cool it," said Hank.

"In that case," said the captain, "we'll have to use Mr. Hennessey's blood."

Hennessey had painted the stripe and dribbled some blood on the outside of the boat as an added fillip and we waited at our posts for the predator to declare himself.

It was a clear mild day, but the ocean was inexplicably choppy, perhaps from some storm recently passed or some foreboding of one to come. The boat, especially at the trolling speed Ugo had set for it, tended to rock back and forth at the pleasure of the waves. We were all at this point a little queasy.

Hennessey was in the worst shape of all, his face drained of color. He was leaning over the deck rail awaiting the call when Ugo stepped out of his cabin.

At first he didn't appear to notice Hennessey although he seemed to be staring at him. After some minutes of this odd, distracted behavior, Ugo brought a bottle of antimotion pills from his cabin and instructed us to take two each without water.

Hennessey could barely get his pills down, then retched them over the side the next moment. Ugo said nothing, merely turned on his heels and marched off. It was not something, you knew, he would easily forgive.

"Didn't do me much good," said Hennessey as soon as he could talk again.

Hank took me aside. "What do you make of his behavior?" he asked.

I pretended to miss his meaning, said *whose* behavior, Hennessey's?

"I think you know who I'm talking about. There is no point in mentioning his name or that we may be dealing

with an acute paranoic suffering from delusions of gran-
deur." All of this was said in a sibilant whisper, a sound not
unlike the lapping of the waves against our hull.

The boat began to lurch more violently than before,
knocking us across the deck and into the railing.

"Battle stations," Ugo called over the loudspeaker.

Hennessey, who had fallen down, was sitting in a puddle
of water, laughing hysterically. Hank was kneeling over
him, whispering I could imagine what in his ear.

"Battle stations," Ugo called again. When we didn't move
he pushed us decisively, each in turn, in the direction he
wanted us to go, shouting some unintelligible command that
sounded like "Birrip, birrip."

"Do you see it?" he cried. He was staring into the ocean,
his gun drawn. "My God, don't you see it?" Two shots
sounded. His thick black hair seemed to be standing on end.

We (I speak for myself at least) saw nothing, only an
opaque and implacable sea, boundless and mysterious, a
mirror without reflection.

"I order you to see it," Ugo shouted. And then we did,
though not before the boat seemed to lift in the air. It was as
if Ugo's gun shots had roused the monster from its deep, had
challenged it into self-declaration. I was not alone in holding
him responsible for its presence.

"You're mad," Hennessey yelled at Ugo or the thing in the
water, one and the other. He had a harpoon in his hand,
though seemed unable to let it go, paralyzed by drink and
terror.

I had never been so frightened in my life and it is unlikely
that I shall ever be as frightened again.

Ugo was leaning over the rail firing his pistol at the spec-
ter of the giant fish.

I had long since disemburdened myself of the harpoon I
had been assigned and it hung like a decoration from the
side of the huge predator.

"Damn you," Hennessey yelled and turning let fly his harpoon at Ugo's head. The shifts and turns of the small boat saved the captain's life for something more in keeping with his obsession to end it. The harpoon caromed blindly off the railing inches from Ugo's shoulder and lodged itself in his shoe.

"Will somebody pull this son of a bitch out," he said, never once taking his eye off the predator. When the pistol was empty he reloaded it and continued his single-minded assault on the moving shock, one or two of his bullets apparently striking home, though to insignificant effect.

He turned to me when his gun was empty a second time and said, "Joshua, the operating manual is in the second drawer on the left in my cabin. I want you to take an oath that you'll get the Discontent II back to port and that you'll tell them, those that didn't make this voyage, what it was like. Can I have your promise here in front of the others?"

I was about to say that my chances of returning were no greater than his—we had already succeeded in unstapling his foot from the deck—when the giant shock leapt from the water to take possession of Ugo's gun hand, removing the weapon at the elbow. The captain's cry was barely heard over the roar of the boat.

He held up his bloody stump like a torch. Where is it gone? he seemed to ask.

Hank, who had fainted, rolled across the deck like a log, one lens of his glasses cracked.

I took out my handkerchief, thinking to bandage Ugo's arm, though it was clearly too late for that. Holding onto the rail to keep my balance, I gave Ugo my word that I would honor his request. The shock was gone, had disappeared beneath the surface, and I remember calling to him in rage and anguish as if he had stolen something from me.

Using his remaining hand, which I clearly remember as the left, Ugo tore the harpoon from his foot. "Stand back," he grunted, a fountain of blood rising miraculously from his boot. His seersucker jacket, what was left of it, had turned a darkening pink. I looked around for Hennessey and didn't see him, called his name three times.

Ugo leaned over the railing, studying the ocean, harpoon drawn back in anticipation, bloody stump inside his jacket. He muttered in Italian, reverting in crisis to the language of his childhood. I had never seen him quite so beside himself.

The waters were mysteriously calm. As unobtrusively as it had come into our lives, the sea monster had returned to the deep, leaving us, as before, as always perhaps, unsatisified.

There was something in the water, flailing about, which I took at first to be the shock returned. Ugo made the same mistake. It is a common illusion to perceive the thing you anticipate despite an opposing reality. The mind is its own place, after all. Still, I make no excuses for Ugo here. He was a man bent on revenging himself, a man, who in all the years I'd known him, had never let the real world intrude on his chimeras.

Ugo flung the harpoon, though the weapon never left his hand. I would never know whether it was Ugo's intention to follow his fling or whether he was unable to let the weapon go. He was a man from the outset, his wife would report, obsessed with holding on to what he had.

There was nothing anyone could do for Ugo after that. His flight was conclusive. He pursued his weapon to its misperceived target.

Ugo and Forster Hennessey rose and fell in the waves, tied together by rope and blood. I threw a life preserver over—it was the least I could do—though neither made any effort to secure it. It was hard to tell whether they were fighting to survive or to destroy the other.

Moments later, the great gray shock, as we had dreamed him, joined them in their final dance.

I did then what I had to do, what Ugo, had he remained in command, would have done himself. I made my way into the cabin and took command of the Discontent II, turning the boat forty-five degrees around so that the nose of the crusier was in the direct line of the three forms in the water. I handled the controls without difficulty and had no doubt, an illusion perhaps though a useful one, that the boat would move exactly as I directed it. The shock was struggling to unseat Ugo who had attached himself to its tail, who in fact seemed to be sodomizing the sea creature, a look of delirious pleasure on his face. When the moment seemed right I drove the boat at full speed at the distracted predator. The creature, though diminished by its wounds, was still a frightening adversary, its eye peering at me with vengeful recognition.

"Don't," screamed Hank from somewhere on the deck. Or perhaps what I heard was the keening of the wind. Once started there was no holding back.

The collision, the shock of impact, knocked me backwards and into an ever receding dark space where monstrous teeth and eye floated over me and under, until I too was in that dance of death with the sea monster and Ugo and Hennessey, the last light of day breaking up in my head like shards of fire.

I had no way of knowing how many hours or days had passed when I came to consciousness again. I was lying in a bunk in the captain's cabin, the surroundings unfamiliar as if erased from memory, a compress on my forehead. Hank was there, sitting next to me, his glasses reduced to one cracked lens, an uncanny effect.

"It's over," he said when he saw that I was awake.

"Is it?"

"It's over and done." That's all that was said, though I have to think that we understood each other as well as we ever had.

What had happened—the details tend to rearrange them-selves each time I look them over—revealed things about and to ourselves we had not been prepared to face.

What remained were the explanations to the authorities and some word or two of condolence to the wives of the deceased. Hank and I worked out a story between us, which had little relation to the real experience, but was less suscep-tible to disbelief.

We invented a reality just incredible enough to give it the ring of arbitrary rightness. In a certain sense, the story I would come to tell made itself up. I take no more credit for it than I do for the accidents of day-to-day experience.

So I told the story. And told the story. I told the story not only to those to whom it had to be recounted but to anyone who would pretend to listen. It got better with each retell-ing, achieved surprises of form, though lost something of its original freshness.

Hank, so the coda to the story goes, became morose and unable to hold a job, became an habitué of certain fashion-able drugs, and drifted, downward step by downward step, into oblivion.

Ugo's wife, Anna, remarried twice within a year, losing husbands and discarding them, and kept a pet snake in a terrarium for her oldest boy, Garo, who talks of becoming a shock-hunter like his old man.

My own life goes on much as before.

I keep telling the story of the shock hunt, revising it as the imagination wills, inventing new possibilities, always veering cautiously from the truth.

And here I told it again, trying with each false variation to make it true.

MR. AND MRS.

McFEELY AT

HOME AND

AWAY

A

Mr. and Mrs. McFeely have had a hard day in the poached preserves of make-believe. When they come home from work (the McFeelys play a version of themselves on *The Mr. Rogers Show* on educational television), they take off their gray wigs and orthopedic shoes and behave just like ordinary people.

"Mrs. McFeely," says Mr. McFeely—they tend to call each other by their last names, a habit picked up from their professional lives—"wouldn't mind putting on the old feedbag if you know what I mean."

"Mr. McFeely, I don't know what you mean," says Mrs. McFeely, rubbing one or the other of her tired feet. "When I come home and take off my shoes I don't want to know what anything means."

"Dear," says Mr. McFeely, changing his seat, unable to sit still, "I'm pleased that you're willing, uh, willing to share your feelings of tiredness with me. On the other hand, I'd like to share my feelings of hunger and general disappointment with you. General disappointment."

"What you need is a little music to soothe the savage beast in you, dear," says Mrs. McFeely. She does a rheumatic shuffle across the room to retrieve her flute case from under a pile of debris. When she returns Mr. McFeely is no longer in the room, has sped away on some imaginary errand, a man with a penchant for making deliveries in the blink of an eye. While Mrs. McFeely does a Mozart solo on the flute, a school of gerbils, apparently entranced by the music, wander into the room followed by two cats, a scrawny dog, and three or four wild geese. Mr. McFeely returns to share his feelings of unrelieved clutter with Mrs. McFeely.

B

The McFeelys tend to watch old home movies before dinner and laugh in a tastefully muted way at their former eccentric behavior.

Look. There is a youthful Mr. McFeely in undersized blue blazer and straw hat paddling a canoe in speeded-up motion. He curls his imaginary mustache for the camera and smiles — surprise! — a grin in which two of his front teeth have been blackened out.

In the next scene we see Mrs. McFeely in ballroom gown and fright wig paddling the same canoe in slow motion.

"Reminds me of the old neighborhood of make-believe," Mr. McFeely says. "Reminds me of it."

In real life, at home in their tastefully furnished suburban tract house, Mr. and Mrs. McFeely laugh at the antics of their former selves.

"Dear, you were simply choice," Mrs. McFeely says.

Mr. McFeely slaps his thigh in amused pleasure. "I was, wasn't I?" he says.

In the next scene, we pick up Mr. and Mrs. McFeely in out-of-focus long shot, standing close together at the edge of a field. The camera zooms in on them, catching them in an awkward embrace from which they extricate themselves the moment they seemingly become aware of the camera's observation. Mr. McFeely turns his back on the camera. Mrs. McFeely giggles girlishly, covers her face with her hands.

"What was going on?" the real-life Mr. McFeely asks.

"I can't imagine what got into us, dear," says Mrs. McFeely. "It's like watching the behavior of complete and utter strangers."

"I'm inclined to think that the man wasn't me at all, but someone dressed up to look like me."

"You're the only one I know who dresses up to look like you," says Mrs. McFeely.

"It wasn't me I tell you. Wasn't me."

"If it wasn't you," says the perturbed Mrs. McFeely, "who on earth could it have been?"

C

After a bout of home movies, the McFeelys move into the kitchen for a spot of dinner. Mr. McFeely, known at Beaver Falls High as Perpetual Motion McFeely, has difficulty sitting in his chair for more than three minutes at a time. He tends to jump up at unexpected intervals and pour Mrs. McFeely a glass of water (or serve her a slice of bread), standing behind her chair with a folded towel over his arm as if he were a waiter in an old-fashioned restaurant. "Aim to please," he likes to say repeatedly. (His idea of a joke is to make the same pointless comment again and again.) Dinner at the McFeelys is not what one expects of it, not at all what one expects. There are no bean sprouts or tofu at their table, no brown rice or dandelion salads. Although the McFeelys value the simple life in the abstract, they tend — Mrs. McFeely is the main offender here — to obsessive behavior. For example, Mrs. McFeely will get a sudden fix on some food like Bird's Eye Hawaiian Vegetables, and for the next several days she will serve nothing but Hawaiian Vegetables for dinner. Guests have been known to complain of the odd fare they've been offered at the McFeelys' table and of the authoritarian behavior of their hosts. No one, as a matter of fact—I'm speaking of both guests and immediate family—is allowed to leave the dinner table at the McFeelys' place until his or her plate is cleaned. The McFeelys believe in maintaining traditional values no matter the personal cost.

D

After dinner, the McFeelys generally have a conversation concerning the events of the day. Some days when nothing much of interest has happened they tend to share make-believe experience. Mrs. McFeely will say something like, "I had a little romance this afternoon with the Man from Glad. He said I had beautiful hands."

"And who," says Mr. McFeely, "was the first postman . . . person to tell you you had beautiful hands?"

Mrs. McFeely has to think about that for a minute or two, a woman, who, if she had the slightest shred of vanity, might pride herself on the accuracy of her responses. "A man named Horace Zeiterfeld from Clittorvile, Indiana was the first," she says. "He presented himself as a glove salesman, though I seriously doubt that that was his real calling."

Mr. McFeely quivers with exaggerated dismay. "I won't say I'm not disappointed," he says cheerfully. "I won't say I'm not. You know how I like to be first at everything."

"I never knew you to be so competitive," says Mrs. McFeely. "My feet, however, are still up for grabs."

"Your feet, dear?"

"To the best of my memory, no one before has ever com-

74

plimented my feet," she says, taking off her right running shoe to make a point. "There's an unmistakeable opportunity for you in the area of feet, Mr. McFeely."

Mr. McFeely clears his throat of conventional impediments. "Your feet, Mrs. McFeely," he says, "are everything they ought to be and more."

"You've won that competition hands down," says Mrs. McFeely.

E

Little is known, if much surmised, as to what the McFeelys do after they retire for the night. If one wonders about their sex life, one wonders in vain. No confidences have reached us from either side. We interviewed a few associates from *The Mr. Rogers Show*—Bob Dog, Purple Panda, Chef Brockett, Daniel Striped Tiger and Henrietta Pussycat—and received mostly blank and disapproving stares to our questions. It was generally supposed that, as Daniel Striped Tiger put it, "The McFeelys would never do anything the least bit improper." We can imagine Mr. McFeely saying, "Wouldn't mind getting it on tonight, dear, if that doesn't interfere with, uh, your integrity as a person." And Mrs. McFeely saying, "If memory doesn't fail me, I believe we got it on two weeks ago Wednesday. Is there any need to repeat the obvious?"

What we do know is this. Mr. McFeely is an insomniac, waking every two or three hours in a state of implacable anxiety. Mrs. McFeely, on the other hand, reports that she can sleep through anything. Mr. McFeely is closely identified with the maxim, Speedy Delivery. Even the most benign lives have their darker sides. Mrs. McFeely reads the same page of *The Women's Room* every night before going to sleep. Human personality is one of the few unsolvable mysteries in our time.

"We are totally ordinary people," Mrs. McFeely insists. "That's the nice thing about us. We are exactly what we seem." She makes faces at the camera when she tells us this, crosses her eyes, lets her tongue protrude fetchingly from the corner of her mouth.

"Oh, I wouldn't say that, dear," Mr. McFeely says when apprised of Mrs. McFeely's remark. "I don't know anyone like us, do you?"

"We are ordinary," says Mrs. McFeely, "in a different way from most ordinary people, but I don't want to make us out as better than anyone else."

"I always felt I was better," says Mr. McFeely when his wife is out of the room.

The truth is, Mr. McFeely leads a secret life. It is so secret that even Mr. McFeely doesn't know exactly what the secret is. The secret eludes him because—one only surmises this— Mr. McFeely is never in the same place long enough to observe his own secret behavior. One conjectures another companion somewhere, someone he visits during his imaginary deliveries for the postal service. A typical conversation between Mr. McFeely and this other person might go as follows.

"Why don't you take a load off your size elevens and have a cup of java," asks the lonely Mrs. Fairchild. "I use an instant that has the smell and flavor of ground roast."

"I really have to run," says the antsy McFeely, jogging in place so as not to let his motor run down.

"If a big strong man like you can't stop an itsy bitsy moment for a hot cup of coffee," says Mrs. Fairchild, "then what's the world coming to?"

They get into double entendre and one thing leads to another. When Mr. McFeely rushes off, he has a sense of having stayed in the same place longer than discretion might warrant. Nevertheless, he has no memory of having done anything that might compromise his reputation for irreproachableness. It is odd, he thinks, that his memory should be so short, but that's the price one pays for living in the future.

When asked about their relationship, Mrs. Fairchild says, "You might say that Mr. McFeely and I have the same bottom line."

It is a provocative remark subject to all kinds of misinterpretation.

Mr. McFeely says, "Mrs. Fairchild knows how to make a man feel at home away from home."

G

Mrs. McFeely is not normally a jealous person, though she can't help but wonder what her husband does with himself when he's not delivering the odd parcel. She has her own work to occupy idle hands: her petit point, her raising and training of gerbils (she has developed a strain capable of inane human communication), her fluting, her English gardening, the occasional poem, her fund raising, her voodoo lessons, her dress designing, her performances on educational television, her pastels, her social work in the neighborhood of make-believe. One day Mr. McFeely comes home with some blond hairs on the collar of his uniform.

"Do you have something to tell me?" she asks him in her most censorious voice.

"Glad as ever to see you, m' love," he says.

She removes one of the blond hairs from his collar and holds it up to the light. "It's not mine," she says. "I can see that much."

Mr. McFeely laughs. "I'd be mighty surprised if it was," he says winking at the unseen camera. "Mighty surprised."

"And what's that supposed to mean I'd like to know?"

77

Mrs. McFeely pouts when angry, keeps her hands crossed in front of her as a defense tactic.

"Just a little joke, dear," he says, popping up from his chair, pacing the room at an exceptional speed. "Just a little joke."

"Sometimes, Mr. McFeely," she says, "I think you have the sense of humor of a goat."

No more is said of the blond hairs and the mystery, if that's what it is, goes temporarily unsolved. Their unacknowledged fight, if that's how it might be described — Mr. McFeely is a man who shies from conflict — is postponed for another day.

H

Is the McFeely's marriage in trouble? One morning, Mrs. McFeely shares her feelings of rejection with her husband by throwing the odd gerbil at him, hitting him between the eyes.

"You could have knocked me over with a feather," says Mr. McFeely after he picks himself up. "Yes sirree, you could have knocked me over and did." He flashes out the door in his mutedly spastic way, and in two hours or so, his business transacted, he is back.

"Funny thing happened to me this morning, dear," he says. "Someone hit me between the eyes with a furry rodentlike animal. I can't for the life of me figure out what they had in mind."

"They may have been angry with you," says Mrs. McFeely.

"There's that of course," he says. "But why would anyone be angry with old Mr. McFeely?" He does a jig while waiting for his wife's response.

"The Gods and Goddesses of Anger," says Mrs. McFeely, "are no respecters of persons."

"I wouldn't be at all surprised," he says. Mrs. McFeely is known for the occasional gnomic remark so Mr. McFeely is not at all put out by the incomprehensibility of his wife's perception. "Thank you for sharing your explanation with me, dear," he says, and speeds out the door before some deity of anger can fling a second gerbil at his head.

I

Mrs. McFeely consults a pretend therapist about the declining fortunes of her make-believe marriage.

The person she consults is an occasional friend of the family, a pretend specialist in the domestic problems of performing artists.

Mrs. McFeely looks uncharacteristically chic for a woman in apparent despair, is wearing a black sweater and dark brown Cacharel pants that in certain light — on her entrance into the therapist's office, for example — offer the illusion of leather.

"Have a seat, Mrs. McFeely," we say, trying at once to be compassionate and unseductive, "and tell us what's on your mind."

"Call me Dora," she says.

Dora it is, though we know for a fact that that's not her real name. After some initial reticence, not unusual in such cases, she mentions the fatal blond hairs.

"Have you had it out with him, Dora?" we ask.

"You sound more like a dentist than a therapist," she says. "I'm afraid if I open my mouth, you'll pull a secret drill out of your pocket." She sniffles, wipes her nose with the back of her sleeve. "Though Mr. McFeely tends to play older men on television, he's always been a bit childish."

"Childish in what way?"

"Childish in the way of being a child. How many ways are there?"

"We mean, Dora, what does Mr. McFeely do that you consider childish?"

She studies the floor for awhile, picks imaginary lint from her sweater. "Well, for one, he rides around the house on a tricycle. Does that qualify as childish in your book?"

"It might be a form of exercise," we say. "Not everything is what it seems."

"I don't know why I came here," she says. "I'm going to leave if you don't mind." She gets up.

J

The whole story comes out. We're not talking about the mysterious blond hairs at the moment, but how the McFeelys got together in the first place.

First of all, they had what we call common interests; they were in the same profession more or less. Second of all, and most tellingly, they had the same last name. Third of all, they were cast as man and wife on the educational television program, *Mr. Rogers*, which made it seem as if their relationship had been determined by some higher power. And then of course they liked each other. There was that.

Once they began to play man and wife—the McFeelys took their commitments with the deepest seriousness—it was difficult to accept something less at the end of the day. Little by little they began to take their make-believe home with them after the show. Mrs. McFeely was an advocate then of what is popularly known as the Stanislavsky Method. She played her character, or so she perceived herself doing, from the inside out. Mr. McFeely, who had always wanted to be a postman and not an actor, who as his wife reports was a trifle childish, tended to confuse art and life. When he played a character he was that character, or as close to it as personality and talent allowed. A student of self-improvement, Mr. McFeely practiced at every available opportunity.

Mr. and Mrs. McFeely at Home and Away

A McFeely maxim: You can never be too good at what you do best.

K

Call it obsession if you will. It comes down to the blond hairs on McFeely's collar. Mrs. McFeely treasures the image like a keepsake. Mr. McFeely can change his jacket or brush the old one clean of foreign hairs, but Mrs. McFeely will continue to see what she sees. She will not forgive Mr. Mc-Feely. He can take the garbage out every day of the week, as he does this day, and she will not give up her anger.

At some point, even Mr. McFeely begins to notice Mrs. McFeely's burgeoning disaffection. She barely acknowledges his presence, never talks to him. None of his tricks of charm—his shirttail hanging out as he rushes back and forth—seem to touch her in the slightest.

"Is something wrong, dear?" he asks. "Something wrong?"

Mrs. McFeely, her hands over her ears, looks around as if wondering where the voice were coming from.

He comes over in his sly quick way and removes one of her hands. "Why won't you answer me?"

"You have no claim on my ears," she says.

Mr. McFeely goes out, consults the oracle of his imagination for advice, and comes back bearing flowers. His wife's unabated anger awaits him at the door. Mrs. McFeely has locked him out and changed the locks.

He knocks at the door until his heart aches, and then he goes wherever despondency will take him.

L

A colleague and friend of the family, Bob Dog appears at Mrs. McFeely's door and implores the aggrieved woman to give her husband the benefit of a second chance. "We all (growl) rate a second chance," he says. "Mr. McFeely is one swell guy."

"What about third chances?" she asks, "and fourth chances? How many chances do you want me to give him?" She is unrelenting, though not without a modicum of self-doubt.

Bob Dog's number concepts begin and end at two, so he is temporarily at a loss for argument. "I have no more to say," he says.

"You see how angry he makes me, Bob Dog," she says. "I can't even be civil to an old friend. How's life treating you, big fellow?"

"As the man with the broken leg says, can't kick," says Bob Dog.

"Did a man with a broken leg really say that?" asks Mrs. McFeely. "That's the kind of remark Mr. McFeely would make."

"Mr. McFeely knows how to cheer a dog up," he says.

"No offense intended, Bob Dog, but you'll be doing us both a disservice if you mention Mr. McFeely's name in this house again."

When Bob Dog leaves with his tail, so to speak, between his legs, Mrs. McFeely wonders if she failed on her social obligations. If she has been remiss, she has no one to blame but the man who has wronged her and gone away without admitting his wrong.

M

To make their marital strife socially useful, the McFeelys acquire two children for the television version of their lives, a boy of twelve (named Dick) and a girl of nine (named Jane). Or is it the other way around? The girl already wears lipstick and a small bra, is exceptionally tall for her age, whatever it is. Or is that not the daughter but the other woman? Nothing is certain in the landscape of make-believe.

They get into a fight over who is to explain the situation to the children. The fight becomes its own object lesson. Mrs. McFeely enunciates the common wisdom: "Sometimes when people don't get along, are fighting too much — you've just seen how awful such a fight can be — it is best for all concerned if they live apart."

The children protest, even cry. They want their mommy and daddy to stay together; they promise not to fight any more or demand things their parents can't afford.

"You simply don't understand," Mrs. McFeely says into the camera. "Our trial separation has nothing to do with anything you've done. We both love you very much. Isn't that so, dear?"

Mr. McFeely wonders how he is supposed to be able to love children he didn't know he had until he arrived that morning at the television studio. "Yes," he says. "That's so."

"Why don't we all hug each other like we used to?" says Dick.

"If you love us," says Jane, "then don't get divorced. Okay?"

Mr. McFeely puts an arm around each of the children. "Just think what a good time we'll have, what a good time, just the three of us doing the town. Tara tara. What do you think of that?"

"It doesn't sound like fun," says Dick. Jane merely shrugs.

A sample Saturday visit is enacted. Mr. McFeely, dressed to the nines, knocks at the door of a simulation of his former house to pick up his two make-believe children. Mrs. McFeely, in the shyest of voices, asks him how he's been getting along. "Just fine and dandy," says the ebullient McFeely. "Just fine and dandy." But we can see from the ravages under his eyes that he is putting up a brave front. "And you?" he asks her. "Oh I'm perfect," she says, looking grim

83

and distracted. The children say good-bye to their mother who says, not quite meaning it, "Have a good time." Everyone is a little subdued except Mr. McFeely, who is a whirlpool of willed energy.

For openers, Mr. McFeely takes the children with him on his delivery route, an experience everyone seems to enjoy despite the revved-up pace. They have pizza for lunch at the Pizza Emporium (a make-believe chain), then they go to a movie which combines entertainment with serious social comment. After the movie they go bowling, look in the window of a toy store, and visit a canning factory. Every moment is filled with unrelenting activity.

"Could we live with you, Daddy?" the children ask. "All Mommy does is sit around the house and complain."

Mrs. McFeely, not to be outdone, takes the children to a museum for the day, buys them posters and other educational materials.

"We're getting used to the new arrangement," the girl called Jane says to the camera. "As my father says, you have to break a few yeggs to make an omelet."

"It's not so bad," says Dick, "but I wish we didn't have to bear the burden for their mistakes."

The McFeelys, in top hat and tie, come out, bow and do a soft-shoe dance on stage together, the credits for the show playing over their faces. The children, among others in the audience, applaud.

N . . .

The McFeelys return home after a hard day performing on *The Mr. Rogers Show*. After a dinner of warmed-over Hawaiian Vegetables, Mrs. McFeely discovers two unaccounted for blond hairs on Mr. McFeely's collar, and the pattern of their lives repeats itself, though only up to the point of Mrs. McFeely sharing her sense of outrage with her husband. After that, the McFeelys' story takes a number of surprising turns. The McFeelys meet, fall in love, fight, marry, divorce, share a life of ascetic deprivation together, meet, go out to dinner, do a soft-shoe dance before an audience, have children, make home movies, meet, fall out of love, play themselves on educational television, fall in love, divorce, raise gerbils, visit a canning factory, pretend to be old, pretend to be young people pretending to be old, pretend to be real, pretend to be make-believe, pretend to express anger, pretend to express a pretense of anger, pretend to share a life together, pretend to a lack of pretension, pretend to meet, pretend to express affection for each other, pretend to be an older couple called Mr. and Mrs. McFeely.

FROM THE

LIFE OF THE

PRESIDENT

The president has to be many places during the day but cannot, as everyone knows, be in more than one place at the same time. For this reason, he has at his disposal a man who bears him a striking resemblance. This is not information known to the general public and is mentioned here in the smallest of voices. The president's surrogate, as he is known in the inner circle, is so much like the president that only experts can tell them apart. It wasn't always that way. In the beginning when the surrogate was first hired, he resembled the president only in physical stature and timbre of voice. In those days he wore a mask of the president's face for public appearances, but later when he grew into the role it was discarded. The mask, we understand, was so presidential that the president liked to wear it himself on occasions when it was useful to seem especially authoritative. After the surrogate grew into his role and was able to discard the mask, the president used it with increasing regularity.

The president, and not his surrogate, is our primary concern, though like some others we have difficulty telling them apart. The president is more sensitive than his imitator, more tentative and self-reflecting. His confidence is not always at its highest point. Little things get the president down, things too unpresidential to mention. He has been trained not to register inappropriate feelings, though his face has been known to betray him. The mask, which is always smiling in a serious and reflective way, is foolproof. The president can be himself beneath the mask, can grimace or cry, while the mask registers a serene presidential confidence. The president's wife, the one and only Madame President, likes the presidential mask at the breakfast table when the president's demeanor is not at its best.

After breakfast the president takes a brisk walk around the presidential grounds accompanied on all sides by secret service operatives. The operatives try to make themselves as unobtrusive as possible, though they tend to be beefy fellows and despite themselves sometimes get in the way. When the president accidentally steps on the heels of the one in front, he tends to ask, "How am I doing?" as a means of distraction. "Better than ever," the man stepped on tends to say, which is something the president appreciates. Like everyone else, the president takes sustenance from approbation. They can see, the president says to himself, that this president is giving one hundred percent of himself. Secret service operatives, like most ordinary citizens, can't help but like a man that's giving his best.

His brisk walk over, the president meets with his morning advisors in the South Room. Each of six advisors has the president's ear for a period not exceeding ten minutes, after which the president draws his own conclusions. Sometimes the president draws no conclusions at all. "The president," one of his morning advisors reports, "has perhaps the most open mind in the free world."

The following is not generally known. The meeting with the morning advisors rarely, if ever, concerns itself with world class problems. Occasionally, when he has more pressing business elsewhere, the president will send his surrogate in his stead. If one allows such distinctions, the president's look-alike is an even better listener than the president. He can listen for hours to almost anything, can find something remarkable in the most banal of statements. "Of course," he will say to an advisor's dreary recitation of biases, "I've been thinking much the same thing myself." The president, on the other hand, tends to be silent, often abstracted, during these morning advisings, his broad mind on the larger issues.

After the morning meeting, the president has a typical lunch of cottage cheese and peanut butter, preferably on separate plates, though sometimes—mostly in periods of crisis—mixed for the sake of convenience. Time being in short supply, the president reads memos while he eats, using them unconsciously (and with a residue of regret) to wipe his hands. A grease stain is a sign of obsessive interest if not wholehearted approval. The surrogate, a meat and potatoes man from childhood, has difficulty mastering the cottage cheese/peanut butter experience, though for the sake of security he has had to tolerate the abominable combination in limited amounts. It is the one aspect of the job that sticks in his craw.

In a self-deprecating moment, the president confides to his wife that he suspects that his surrogate is better loved by the people than he is himself. "He can afford to be nice," says the president ruefully (he has had one vodka too many on this occasion). "None of it is real to him."

"Not all the people love him better," says the first lady, "because I don't love him better. There's no question in my mind that you're the superior president."

"I am the only president," says the president, wondering if he has stated the case more strongly than necessary.

After lunch, the president takes a short nap at his desk, twenty-five to thirty minutes. When he wakes—usually an aide wakes him by shaking his shoulder—he does a series of stretching exercises for his back. Refreshed and strengthened, he then meets with his afternoon advisors who brief him on the major trouble spots in the world.

From the Life of the President

Nothing gives him more pleasure than the high level give and take of crisis negotiations. This is presidential work, this is why he entered the lists for the top job in the first place. The president is forceful with his afternoon advisors, lets them know who's running the show in case anyone has other ideas. The more brilliant the advisor is, the better educated, the more dangerous his ambitions. Afternoon advisors tend from time to time to forget their place, which is something the president will not tolerate. A man in the president's employ, who forgets his place, may suddenly find himself out of place, displaced, in a place in the shade. Something else the president will not tolerate is to have his surrogate replace him at the afternoon policy meetings. Crises, the president will write to himself in a note, are matters too serious to be left to the shadow of one's self.

After lunch, while the president conducts matters of state, his surrogate speaks to visiting dignitaries, to women's clubs, to union leaders, to civil liberties groups, to Boy Scouts, to ambassadors from countries of limited political significance, does whatever small offices the president is unable to perform in his own person. The surrogate, a man of neither brilliance nor ambition, is pleased to be of use.

After the meeting with the crisis advisors, the president sits alone in the dark, considering some or all of the important issues of the day. The president, who is a Zen enthusiast, lets the decision come to him (like a light in the tunnel) rather than the other way around. The president prides himself on his ability to make decisions for which afterward he has only the most negligible regrets. As the first lady has been known to say, the president can live with his less inspired decisions as well as the next man.

After the president comes out of the dark, he signs bills into laws for the next fifteen or twenty minutes. The president, who writes a beautiful hand, enjoys the signings almost as much as his world class meetings with the crisis advisors. The president's signature is as much admired for its calligraphic qualities as for its firmness of line.

The signings completed, the president has a brief liaison with one of his three mistresses in the Illicit Room. The president has committed himself each day to this thirty or forty minute interlude as a way of keeping in touch with the tenderer side of his nature (or as a way of exorcising a potential excess of tenderness). It is rumored that, on that rare occasion, when the president is in no mood for sex—he is, after all, not indefatigable—he sends his surrogate in his place to entertain whatever mistress is on tap for that day. Though the identities of the president's mistresses is classified information, it is known that none is as beautiful as the president's wife. The president is opposed to elitism and so chooses his mistresses from the national pool of ordinary women, the heart and soul of his constituency. If the mistresses were beautiful or fascinating, the president might find himself in danger of losing his head.

In the evening (not every evening but this one), the president gets into an extended disagreement with his wife. It goes like this.

"I hate living without any privacy," she complains over dinner. "One of the secret service men was looking at my breasts through the kitchen window; perhaps he thought they were time bombs. I really wish you had never run for president."

"You encouraged me to run if you remember."

"And you told me, if *you* remember, that I had the moral scruples of a Lady Macbeth. You even suggested that if I wanted a president in the family, I ought to run myself."

The proximity of secret service men mutes the intensity of these exchanges, though at the same time gives the president and his wife an audience for their grievances.

The president tends to wake during the night, stirred from dreams by the most inconspicuous sound. The chirp of a cricket in the next county can bring him to his elbows. Sometimes when he wakes, he stares into darkness thinking about baseball or childhood. Other times he ruminates about matters of state.

The president's wife almost never wakes before nine unless the president himself wakes her. Not at her best when shaken from sleep, she is nevertheless one of the world's foremost middle of the night listeners. Madame President, as her husband calls her, has the enviable capacity, perhaps acquired in marriage, perhaps inborn, of being able to hold a high level conversation in her sleep. So when the president wakes during the night with matters of state on his mind, he tends to consult his wife without actually waking her.

THE PRESIDENT'S WIFE GIVES THE PRESIDENT AN IDEA

This morning, in a press conference, the president announced that starting tomorrow everyone in his employ would wear a tie and coat during working hours. The president said his wife had suggested the idea as a gesture against the moral disintegration of society. The president quoted his wife as saying, "If we could get the whole world to wear ties and coats, I think everyone would behave in a more respectable way. It might even make human nature take a turn for the better."

While the president is announcing the new dress code, the president's surrogate, dressed in coat and tie, visits the president's wife.

"The president," says his look-alike, "has asked me to entertain you while he carries his message to the nation."

"Did he really?"

"Not really. I had to have an excuse to come and see you, so I made that one up."

91

Madame President, who is a stickler for protocol, asks for a clarification. "This isn't an official visit then, is it? I want to get that cleared up right away. You're here for reasons that have nothing to do with official government policy."

"I am self-propelled in this instance," says the surrogate. "I am at the mercy of some newly announced internal authority."

The president's beautiful wife blushes at the words "internal authority." "You should leave, I think," she says. "Don't you think?"

The president's impersonator has difficulty making decisions, says he will leave if she really wants him to leave.

"I think I've made my position clear," says the first lady.

The alternative president bows his head, would confess his unrequited love, though can't find the words. Instead he says, "I had no assignment for this hour and I've gotten so used to doing the things he does, I thought I'd drop in on his private life to see what I could learn from it."

"It's a free country," she says. "The president has impressed the fact on me whenever I appeared to think otherwise."

"What would the president say to you now," says the surrogate, "if he were in my position?"

"Oh, the president!" exclaims his wife. "He would do exactly what you're doing, though with not quite so much reticence."

"That's exactly the kind of thing I need to know," says the surrogate.

"There's no one so good at what he does, the president always says to me, that he can't become better at it," says the president's lady with borrowed sententiousness.

The surrogate takes a seat at the maximum distance from the first lady before speaking again. "I may be out of line in saying this," he says, "I may be far afield as we say in debriefing sessions, but. . . ."

The president's wife is touched by the man's reticence and indicates that he could talk to her as he would to any of the president's advisors. "What should I call you?" she asks him.

"The others call me Mr. President, though that may be a bit awkward for you."

She waves off his objection. "What do you wish to ask me, Mr. President?"

"Is there a kind of experience, real or imaginary, that touches you to the heart?"

"The death of a small dog always makes me cry," she whispers, looking away. In recollection of such pathos, a tear escapes.

"Do you find morning, afternoon, or evening the most attractive part of the day?"

"No preference."

"Do you remember your childhood with a sense of overwhelming loss?"

"I have no recollection of childhood."

He jumps up from his chair and says, "Oh how alike we are, Doris."

Madame President holds out her arm to ward off the imposter. "I'll have to ask you to leave if you can't control yourself," she says. "You must never let yourself forget that the woman in front of you is your Commander-in-Chief's wife."

"I couldn't love you if you weren't," says the president's other self. "It's my business to be as much like the president as is humanly possible."

The outcome of this interview has a certain inevitability.

The false president moves by degrees into the real wife's good graces. He sits next to her on the presidential love seat, tells her of his vision of peace and prosperity, holds her hand.

The illicitness of their relationship adds a charge to this otherwise innocent encounter.

That evening, the president mentions that he is thinking of removing the surrogate, who has begun to forget his place. What does Madame President think?

The timing is so odd. The first lady finds the question vaguely accusatory and consequently insulting. She averts her lovely gray eyes, says nothing.

"The real problem is what to do with him once we remove him," says the president. "It might be a little sticky having him wandering around telling his story to whoever comes along. The fact is, the fellow knows too much."

The president's wife blanches. "You'll have to get him to promise not to say a word. You can get your lawyer, can't you, to make up some document that will enjoin the guy to silence."

"We can't rely on promises in matters of national security," says the president. "The fellow must, as we say at the highest level of policy discussion, disappear permanently."

When she realizes that the president has the unimaginable in mind she puts her hand to her breast and sighs.

That night, too distraught to sleep, she argues for the life of the surrogate, employing her usual high level of subtlety, urging (as she often does) the opposite of what she really wants. The president takes her advice at face value, further convinced that the course of action he leans to is the correct one. If the leader of a country can't make the unpopular decisions, who can?

On the advice of another of his trusted counselors, the president has a meeting with his surrogate, which is recorded by secret microphone.

"What are your aspirations, fella?" the president asks him, getting to the point without the usual delay.

The surrogate, trying to understand the question in its proper context, can only assume that the first lady has betrayed him. "To be of service to the president," he says.

"Yes, yes," says the president, looking at his watch, "but

when such service is concluded—it can't go on forever, can it?—what kind of career would you like to pursue?"

The surrogate doesn't know, hasn't thought about anything beyond his immediate responsibilities.

"You haven't thought of replacing me, have you?" asks the president.

"Sir," says the surrogate, "if you want my resignation, you have only to ask for it."

"You've become so much like me, you seem to be able to anticipate my thoughts."

The surrogate smiles faintly. "I've gotten too good at my job, is that it?"

The president glances off into the presidential mirror, confuses the other's image momentarily with his own. "Nothing lasts forever," he says in his presidential voice. "I'd like to know for my own peace of mind what you plan to do next."

The surrogate says that he plans to take it easy for a while, spend some time with family and friends, get to know himself better, and explore whatever options are available.

The answer does not sit well with the president, though it is an answer he himself has given in the past and will, when the circumstances warrant, give again in the future. "The interview is concluded," he says curtly.

One day the surrogate leaves the president's service and the next day no more is heard from him.

A month or so later, the president wakes during the night in a state of extreme anxiety. "Doris," he asks his sleeping wife, "has my life taken a false turn?" He gets no answer, not even the barest murmur of denial. In the darkness, he perceives the outline of a figure that resembles him. It is my own ghost, he thinks. The text of the face in front of him is unyielding, though he leans forward in an attempt to penetrate its disguise. Either the shadow moves closer or the perceiver moves closer to the shadow. The surrogate, he discovers, is himself.

The president has no surrogate. He has dreamed the surrogate as he dreams the routine of his day, as he dreams his wife next to him who answers his questions in her sleep, as he dreams the power and glory of his office. The president is his own surrogate, a chameleon of a man, a man of different selves for different occasions. The president's life is a succession of dreams or the same dream repeated over and over with slight variation; he starts out in this dream with a sense of high purpose, a belief in his ability to be a force for good, a feeling of having an enviable destiny, and ends with self-betrayal and murder. He wakes from one dream to another and from that dream to the next and so has the illusion of a life.

THE HONEST

COMPANY

I am in the city of my birth, walking with a journalist from out of town on the way to an appointment with a woman I haven't seen in something like fifteen years. The journalist is there to interview me, though he has run out of questions. We pass a bookshop in which I notice the literary historian Alfred Fitzpatrick Boone browsing at the remainder table. He has the odd habit of removing a book and studying the spine before glancing at the text. It strikes me that my visitor would get pleasure from meeting the nineteenth-century scholar, and I offer him the opportunity. "Yes," he says, "I would like that. I quite like his book on Smart." As we return to the bookstore, I wonder if Al will mind our intruding on him, and until the introduction is actually made, I regret my impulsiveness. Al is gracious in his characteristically distracted way, says he is pleased to see me again, has heard a great deal of me over the years. In fact, he says (he goes to another table and brings over a pile of brochures) he has just seen some broadsides that mention my name. He is extremely polite and presents the pile of literature to me to look through while he talks to my visitor.

My pleasure in his behavior collapses as I glance at the brochure that tops the pile and notice my name running through it in one derogatory context after another. The brochure is put out by a company called Honest Services, and from what I can make out on cursory examination, I am

97

the negative example in a set of dialogues—the devil's advocate (and straw man) against whose arguments the Honest spokesman is shown to triumph. The speaker using my name is presented as vulgar and calculating, as self-deluded if not unequivocally dishonest. What right do they have to use my name this way? I consider possible remedies, including, I say with some embarrassment, the banality of legal action. In italics near the top of the brochure there is a disclaimer that reads: "Joshua Quartz is a composite name and not a real person." Nonsense! I am the only Joshua Quartz in the phone book.

On closer inspection, I discover that the brochures are styled as questionnaires. "Do you agree with J.Q., or do you agree with the Honest Speaker?" the text asks disingenuously. There are boxes in the margins for comments. I can't resist reading through the forms to see what these respondents from all walks of life have to say about me. Someone, I notice, has agreed with me (or my namesake) throughout the second page of the brochure. It is odd, but I am actually cheered by the quixotic support and turn to the first page to see the name of this singular ally. "I. M. Spoof," he or she has written at the top of the page. At the first reference to my name, the respondent has scribbled over it, "a sissy name." The remark does not ingratiate itself.

The Company is being willfully deceitful—can there be any doubt?—when they allege that my name is a composite. Willful and malicious deception is my charge against them. I make a long-distance phone call to my lawyer, who is in another city at the moment, pursuing some lucrative chance. I consider what I might sue for, moving between a million dollars, which would permit retirement, and the more honorable satisfaction of a public apology. I see myself refusing the offer of money and accepting nothing less than a complete and unequivocal retraction. One's honor has no price.

Vengeance must be performed with the grace of disinterested surgery.

My lawyer doesn't seem to know what my rights are in this matter and says he will need some time to check, to give him a number he can reach me at night and day. He is famous, this lawyer, and high priced, and yet he has no information at hand. The simplest query requires months of study. He is constantly learning, he likes to say, making a virtue of appalling ignorance. To hire him is to subsidize his education. I don't expect to get his answer until his answer is no longer of use. When I get back to the bookshop, Al is there by himself, browsing in his intent, self-absorbed way. My visitor has gone without remarking on his destination. "I think I inspired him," says Al, "to see the city on his own steam." I return the questionnaire to Al, keeping one back for evidence, and ask what he thinks of the Honest Company using my name in this abusive way. Al seems surprised at my anger, having assumed, he says, that my name was used with my consent. Or that on some occasion I had actually said the things attributed to me. "It must be an honest mistake," he says. "The company has an impeccable reputation."

"It's the kind of reputation," I say, "that if there's any justice, will receive its ultimate reward in hell." My vehemence exceeds intention.

"How can you condemn another human agency," Al says in the voice of sweet reasonableness, "without giving them a hearing first? One must proceed with caution and generosity. There are any number of possible explanations for the ostensible mischief of these brochures, including, if I may say so, the honest mistake."

My outrage is not so easily assuaged. Would he be so dispassionate if it were his name in the brochure and not mine? I find myself overstating a case that needs nothing but the barest enunciation to seem undeniable.

"There is a mystery here," Al says, "and it won't be uncovered until we query the Honest people themselves."

In such fashion I learn that we are to go together to the Honest Company headquarters.

2

We take a cab, which Al hails with a snap of his fingers. "Take us to the Honest Company factory," he says, giving out an address as if he knew it by heart. The scruffy driver is indifferent to Al's directions, takes a circuitous route.

"Don't worry, I know what I'm doing," the driver says in answer to my unspoken complaint. "In a certain sense, if you follow me, all roads lead to the same inevitable place. Am I right?"

Al sits back with his hands folded behind his head. "I have learned," he says, "that chance plays an important part in human affairs. I never think myself lost."

"Look at it this way," says the driver. "We may be the only ones that aren't lost."

The neighborhood we pass through is in terminal disrepair, shops boarded up, houses burned to the ground, tiny fragments of glass glimmering like jewels along the sidewalks. It goes on and on, this country of desolation. Occasionally, we see a starving cat, or two or three ragged children scavenging in the dust.

We come to an unexpected stop. "This is your destination," the driver says. "The Bonnet Warehouse. It's been closed for five years, but when I set my mind to it I can find anything."

Al seems prepared to get out, and I put my hand on his shoulder to stay his move. "This is the wrong place," I say.

I can see the driver's scowl in the front mirror and anticipate further difficulty. "It's a poor passenger that blames his taxi," he mutters.

"We asked to be taken to the Honest Factory," I remind him.

"You'll have to pay for this fare before I can set off on another. It's the rules of the Company."

"Is it in the Company's rules that the passenger pay for the driver's mistake?" I say, making my tone as conciliatory as possible. "We specifically asked to be taken to the Honest Factory."

"And I took you there, right? The Honest Factory has changed its name to the Bonnet Warehouse."

"He has you there," says Al, who, for an apparent ally, seems to be on the other side more often than not.

Al takes a sheaf of bills from his wallet and pays the driver considerably more than his fare.

The confusion over place continues to trouble me. If the Bonnet Warehouse has been closed for five years (and that seems the only indisputable piece of information), how is it possible for the demonstrably functioning Honest Company to have metamorphosed into this defunct organization?

"Nothing surprises me any longer," says Al.

Al gets out of the taxi and I reluctantly follow him, asking the driver to wait a few minutes for us if he would. His shrug is without commitment. When we turn our backs he drives away, stranding us in this wasteland from which every civilized human being has fled.

Al knocks with authority at the warehouse door. The sound of clanging chains echoes back, the hammering of metal against metal. It indicates some life inside, and we wait with our backs to the building for someone to release the sliding door. Al knocks again and then a third time.

"What's the pitch?" calls a voice like a bullfrog's.

"We're looking for Bonnet's Warehouse," says Al.

Gradually, the large door lifts open, jerking and wheezing as it rises, to reveal a dark cavernous space.

A squat old man struggles slowly into the light. "Who wants Bonnet's" he asks.

"We're looking for the Director of Bonnet's Warehouse," Al says. "Is it the least bit possible that we're talking to that party at this moment?"

The old man seems momentarily blinded by the gray light of this cloudy afternoon. "I'm very busy at this time of year," he says. "I suppose you want to see the man in charge. Is that what you want?"

Al acknowledges that it is.

"There are no calls these days for the lesser lights," the old man grumbles. "It's a symptom of the time, if you ask me. Everyone wants to start at the top. May I ask the nature of your business with Mr. Bonnet?"

"This gentleman," Al says, nodding in my direction (I have been standing sideways, slightly behind him, looking around for another cab), "feels that he's been misrepresented in one of your publications."

"I can't believe what I've heard," the old man mumbles. "If you can't trust your own ears, you might as well give up the game."

"It may be we've come to the wrong place," I say. "We're under the impression that the Honest Company has changed its name to Bonnet's Warehouse."

A gleam of light crosses the old man's face as if it had nowhwere else to go. "What name do you go by?" he asks me.

I am reluctant to give it out and look over at Al to get his advice. There is no advice forthcoming. Al is staring into the sightless distance, distracted by the unfathomable.

"Did I miss something?" the old man asks, picking at the wax in his ears.

I mumble my name unintelligibly.

"When you have something to say, we'll talk about it," he says, looking over at Al. "Perhaps the issue of misrepresentation hides more than it reveals." At that, he turns and withdraws into the dark space behind.

"I believe he means us to follow him," says Al, hunching under the descending door.

Al has a talent for comprehending the unspoken, and so on faith—besides there is nowhere else to go—I follow my guide inside the dimly lit warehouse. The door closes behind us with a bang.

There are several old cars in advanced states of disrepair lying about in the cavernous anteroom, a sign on one of the walls (as we pass): WORK AREA—ADMITTANCE RESTRICTED TO AUTHORIZED PERSONNEL. At one point we come across the hollowed-out front ends of five cars piled one on top of another like pieces of interlocking puzzle.

"What do you make of all this?" I ask Al.

"Typical," he says sagely.

"I suppose Bonnet's had been in the car repair business at some time," I say.

"Yes and no," confides my advisor. "These old family businesses have always had a few extra cars in their garages."

Although we have lost sight of the old man—he has gone through some door in the back—Al advances with authority and I follow his lead.

We take a service elevator to the fifth floor, an ancient machine that makes a gasping sound, a seeming death throe, at each landing. Al stands by the 40-watt light bulb, reading a book as we painstakingly ascend.

When we get out of the elevator on the fifth floor there is a large desk in the hall with a receptionist sitting behind it. "Can I help you?" this woman of a certain age asks with great sweetness, the offer seemingly more than perfunctory.

"We are here to see Mr. Bonnet," says Al.

"Mr. Bonnet is in conference," she says with infinite regret. "Please take a seat."

"How do we know this is the right place?" I whisper to Al when we've taken our seats.

103

"It's my guess that it is," says Al. "In any event, what we're after is a symbolic gesture, isn't it? One is as good as another."

I return to the desk to ask the receptionist a question, have difficulty gaining her attention. After a few minutes she looks up and makes a noise of surprise. "I'm so sorry," she says in her sweet voice. "I didn't see you standing there. How can I make it up to you?"

I whisper my obsessive question. "Is there something called the Honest Company or Honest Factory in this building?"

"Honest as in honest?" she asks. Her phone rings and she picks it up with mechanical dispatch. "Two men," she says in answer to a question. "They've been waiting for the longest time and I think you ought to see them at your convenience." She winks at me. Something further is said on the other end—it sounds like the growl of a dog—and she returns the receiver to its rest. "Mr. Bonnet will see you," she says. "Do you know the way? You go down the corridor about thirty yards then take a left turn. Actually, it doesn't matter which way you turn. Mr. Bonnet is in the third office on the right side."

"Didn't he used to be the fourth office on the left side?" asks Al.

She thinks about it, nervously twirling a curl around her pencil. "Oh, that was the senior Mr. Bonnet," she says.

"And he's no longer in charge?" I ask.

"I'm not in a position to say," she says. "Is it the father you want or the son?"

I look to Al for advice, but his attention is centered on the receptionist to the exclusion of all else.

I have difficulty with decisions, tend to regret them moments after the fact. "We'll see the younger Mr. Bonnet," I say quickly, letting the choice happen of itself, "the one that's expecting us."

"I hope you know what you're doing," she says, her apparent doubt intensifying mine.

Al reaches across the desk and acquires the receptionist's hand as if he were picking up a pencil. "You have beautiful eyes," he says. "They're an astonishing shade of blue."

"They're brown," she says sadly.

"I was speaking in metaphor," he says.

We go down a long corridor, Al in the advance, make a number of intricate turns (more, I suspect, than required), pass two watercoolers, to an unoccupied office that is apparently Mr. Bonnet's. I retrieve outrage. Why isn't the man here to receive us? Al falls asleep in his chair or merely sits back with his eyes shut. Finally—it is just when I am thinking of trying another office—a man of about my own age arrives.

"Sorry," he says, "but nature called." The hand he offers to confirm our meeting is slightly damp, has a mildewed aspect.

I have an appointment, temporarily forgotten, somewhere else in the city and feel constrained to conclude this business quickly. The question is where to begin. Al, who has been my spokesman, is no longer of use, is asleep in his chair, mouth ajar, arm across his face as if to ward off blows. I take a brochure from my jacket pocket and pass it to Mr. Bonnet across the desk. "Have you seen this before?" I ask.

"Good stock," he says, feeling the paper between his fingers before studying the text. "Uh huh," he murmurs. "Uh huh." He puts a jeweler's glass to his eye. "The work is good, quite good, but not perfect, not without the taint of flaw."

"I don't know if I'm in the right place," I say. "Is . . . "

He interrupts. "Of course you're in the right place."

"It's the text I'm concerned about," I say.

"As you might be, as you no doubt are," says the apparent

105

younger Bonnet. "In my view, one text is no better nor worse than another. I like them all and have no use for any."

I can't seem to explain myself. Words refuse my tongue, take refuge in inaccessibility. "Are you Honest?" I hear myself ask.

"That's one of those questions," he says. "If I affirm it, I in effect deny it. If I deny it, I by implication affirm it. Sir, I suspect you are trying to trap me into an answer I am unwilling to give."

At this point, Al opens his eyes to the world. "Like Homer," he says, "even I sometimes nod."

I ask Al to explain the situation to Mr. Bonnet, to make our position unambiguous.

Al considers my request for a moment or two, gleaning whatever text the room yields to his scholarly eye. "I suspect Mr. Bonnet has heard enough," he says. "He understands our position. It's not appropriate nor gentlemanly to say more than enough. Would you subscribe to that, Mr. Bonnet?"

"I am at your service, gentlemen," says our host. "I will do as much as I can, but no more, need I say, than is just."

"That satisfies me," says Al, standing up and offering his hand. "That's as fair as can be said."

All of this is too oblique for my taste. I want to know what specific steps Mr. Bonnet's elusive firm means to take on my behalf and am about to say something to that effect.

Mr. Bonnet gets up to accompany us to the door. "It's been a pleasure, gentlemen," he says.

"I find the brochure intolerable," I say. Al's face collapses in pain and I would give my life to recall this graceless remark. "Of course you do," says Mr. Bonnet, and then we are in the long corridor again, the door closed behind us.

Al stops at the second watercooler for a drink. "He's behaved well," he says. "Don't you think so?"

The Honest Company

Embarrassed to admit to Al that I can conceive of no basis for judgment, I say nothing, withhold the hypocrisy of a nod.

"I'll catch up with you downstairs," says Al. "I have some unfinished business to discuss with the front desk."

Riding down alone in the service elevator, I am hit by the full burden of my dissatisfaction. (Grievance is never so sharp as when it remains unshared.) The elevator rocks from side to side as it descends in its infinite languor.

A woman is waiting for me in another part of the city, is waiting or has gone, our appointment long passed, thirty or forty minutes in arrears. If I hadn't seen Al in the window of the bookstore, if I hadn't retraced my steps to introduce him to my visitor, I would have been in front of the Paragon Hotel at the appointed time. She is an old friend, this woman, someone I haven't seen or corresponded with in fifteen years. The elevator is painfully slow, unbearably halting. I decide to get off at the next floor, which is the third, and walk the remaining distance, walk or run. It takes some time for the elevator to stop and still more time for it to open its doors.

The third floor, like the fifth, has a large receptionist's desk facing the elevator.

I ask the young woman on duty where the stairwell is, am asking her when I notice a stack of familiar brochures on the corner of the desk.

"You can take one if you like," she says.

When she isn't looking I stuff a handful into my jacket pocket, wanting to put as many out of circulation as possible. "Miss, who puts these out?" I ask.

"To tell you the honest truth, I don't know," she says. "I found them this morning when I came in." She picks up a brochure and reads it to herself, smiling at certain lines. "Choice," she says from time to time.

There are some posters on the wall behind her head, surfers and Spanish dancers and young lovers on golden beaches under the bloodshot eye of the sun, but there is no indication of the name of the firm.

"Is this the Honest Company?" I ask abruptly.

"Pardon?"

I don't get to repeat the question as a squat old man, the very one that let us into the warehouse, comes over with an air of borrowed urgency. "I need five thousand of these by tomorrow," he says to the girl, tossing a thick brown envelope into her In box.

"I've been waiting for you," he says to me. "I was afraid you'd gotten swallowed up."

In his small cluttered office, he pours us both a drink of some evil-smelling liqueur called Pastis. He downs drink after drink, as though spilling the stuff out the window, suffering it with his eyes closed, coughing and sputtering. At some point, he knocks a sheaf of papers onto the floor to make room for his arms. "Shall I tell you why you came to see me?"

"I came to see you because of this brochure," I say.

"You came to see me because of this brochure," he says. "Is that it?"

The kindness of his manner makes my anger seem ungenerous.

"And what can we do to make it right?" he asks.

I am disarmed, can think of nothing that's not excessive or insufficient or a combination of both. "What do you think?" I ask.

He takes a handkerchief from the inside of his coat and mops his forehead. "We're prepared to do one of two things," he says. "The first would be to offer you a generous sum of money and a private apology in exchange for a signed release. Not what you would want, I should think. Not what I would want if I were in your moccasins, young man.

The second thing, and I would be less than honest if I didn't tell you it was my preference of the two, would be for the Honest Furniture Company to make a public apology for the unauthorized use of your name. The only drawback to that, as I can see, is that it might call renewed attention to the original and so, in some quarters at least, have the reverse effect of its intention." He folds his hands across his stomach and leans back in his chair.

I am aware, of course, that the second alternative is preferable, but it doesn't (haven't I been through this all before?) undo the harm already done.

"Of course, you'll need some time to think about it," he says. "I don't want to rush you into a decision you'll regret." He stands up as if he means to leave.

"I'm already late for another appointment," I say.

"In that case" (he hands me his card), "why don't you call me tomorrow morning and let me know your decision."

He leads me to his private elevator, which is as fast, he assures me with a paternal hand on my shoulder, as the other one is dilatory. We shake hands like old friends. "The next time give me a little warning, and we'll have lunch together." he says.

The speed of the elevator forestalls disillusion. I reach the ground floor in the blink of an eye. Not finding Al, I assume that he's gone on without me, assuming as he might that I had gone on without him.

3

As I ride in a taxi through rush hour traffic, my elation dims. I've wasted hours over nothing. What difference to my life if the Honest Company makes a public apology or doesn't. The damage is already done or not done, is no considerable damage in any event. A triviality provoked me. My anger and outrage were in excess of the provocation, were themselves trivalities. As a consequence, I'm more than politely late for an appointment I had every intention of keeping, that increases in importance with each renewed delay. Fifteen years ago in another city I had been in love with this woman, had been mad for her, suffering the moments apart like a duration in hell. It had been the same for her, or seemed so. We had separated—I forget the reasons, I know the reasons but refuse to remember them—had suddenly found ourselves living three thousand miles apart. For several months we had exchanged letters, and then she moved again, or I did, and we had lost contact. She had stopped writing first—that much I remember—but that she had was my fault, something I had said in one of my letters or not said, a failure of commitment or sensibility. I had been married then. She too. It was a time in which people believed in staying married no matter what for the sake of the children or for the sake of marriage itself. In those days having made one's bed, one felt obliged to sleep in it, broken springs and all. The woman, who had no children, not then, eventually separated from her husband. I stayed with my family and wrote the woman love letters without mentioning the word love. At some point her letters seemed to cool, became more guarded and discreet, and then stopped altogether. My memory is faulty. The letters never cooled. What happened was that the intervals between letters became greater and greater until one had the illusion that the letters were no longer being written. I made no attempt to find the woman. There was a war on at the time, which was the excuse I offered myself, one of many. I assumed that we would pick up where we left off when the war was over, assumed that or something like it. I no longer remember my assumptions or may not have had any. I consoled myself with the view that there was nothing I could have done to dissuade her disappearance. If I had no word of her over the years, or almost none (I heard once from some mutual friend that she had married a second time), I had fleeting glimpses of her, or imagined I did, in a passing car, in the window of a restaurant, in the waiting room of an airport. She had been greatly changed by the years almost unrecognizably changed. She had been reduced by the imagination to a faded apparition of a fading memory. If she existed for me at all, it was as an endlessly transformable conjecture, a different face for different seasons. That was the case until three weeks ago when I received a note in her hand saying she would be in my city on the twenty-third of June and could we meet in front of the Paragon Hotel at four in the afternoon. The postmark on the letter was illegible. There was no return address. What an odd request after fifteen years, I thought, and all the more mysterious for having come from nowhere. The note offered no explanation for the meeting and no information about her life during the intervening years, offered nothing beyond the time and place of our presumed appointment. One resists such peremptory requests. I decided I didn't want to see her, and then I did an about face and decided I did, curious to see what she had become (and to see what I had become in her eyes). And that's where I was going when I happened to see Al Fitzpatrick Boone in the window of the bookshop and Al happened to show me the infamous brochure.

The cab is stopped at a red light, the driver writing something in a notebook as he waits for the signal to change. Horns blare from the row of cars behind. The driver, who bears a family resemblance to the one who took us to Bonnet's Warehouse, continues writing, seemingly oblivious to the grievances of those trapped by his inertia.

"The light has changed," I report.

The driver raises his shaggy head, mumbles something, then returns to his chore. "I was in the middle of a sentence," he announces somewhat petulantly when the sentence has been concluded. The light turns red before we can

111

move from the spot. The driver takes his pen from his shirt pocket and returns his attention to the notebook in his lap.

"I'm in a hurry," I say. "Please don't start another sentence."

"I'm just repairing the old one," he says.

"Are you working on a novel?"

"It's a broadside. A commissioned job."

After this discussion, we move at a slightly better pace, weaving in and out, edging between and around the obstructions of rush hour traffic. A red light stops us a half block from my appointed destination, and I consider getting out and walking to the hotel. Instead, I hear myself say, "I'd like to ride slowly by the hotel and get out at the next corner."

Without looking up from his manuscript, the driver mumbles his acknowledgement.

There's no reason to expect that she'll have waited two hours for me and I caution myself against hope. As we approach the hotel, my face is pressed against the glass of the window. There are several people going in and out of doors, another cab stopped just ahead. A small woman and a blond child of about four get in the cab. The woman with the child might be her. Standing just to the side of the entrance is an older woman with silver hair, a lap dog and handbag at her feet, her face paralyzed with displeasure. I am a believer in unrecognizable transformations, though refuse this one. Fifteen years is not an eternity. (I take a comb from my jacket pocket and straighten my hair, which is thinner than it was and streaked with gray.) A woman emerges from the swinging doors just as we pass, a tallish woman, slightly stooped, her face ashen. She looks everywhere but at the cab, which is moving relentlessly, my face at the window, toward the far corner. The woman is exceptionally handsome, quite striking in an unannounced way, her face lived in as other faces gives the impression of having only been visited. I can't be completely sure that she is the one I am there to meet, have only that transitory image to consider, that unfocused, vanishing photograph. I try her name on my tongue, speak it silently.

The cab slides by the corner, doesn't stop. Does he know something I don't? "Did I tell you to go on?" I hear myself saying. And we go on, tearing ahead, leaving three streets behind before we come to another red light. I imagine throwing open the door and running back to the hotel, but in a moment we are moving again. "Stop here, will you?" I call to him. My appeal has the impact of silence. He goes on and on, the illuminated city fleeing in the distance. His momentum carries him through a succession of interchangeable suburbs and finally toward the embankment of a river. "What went wrong?" I ask him. He takes his hands from the wheel and shows them to me as if they were evidence of good faith. I have a sudden terrifying insight. "You're employed by the Honest Company, aren't you?" He doesn't deny it.

We go on and on until the lights of the city glimmer faintly in the distance like the aura of a forgotten life.

CHILDREN OF

DIVORCED

PARENTS

I was hung up on my first wife, Marie, for a long time, as a consequence, I suspect, of having been thrown over by her. There may be other explanations, but I have always been partial to the obvious. Marie's disaffection, twenty-three years ago to the month, remains one of the indelible facts of my life. Whoever else I am, I am also the man that Marie no longer wanted. The note she left me in lieu of herself explained her position with merciless clarity. "I see no future for us," she wrote. "You're not the man I want to spend the rest of my life with under the same roof."

Three years later when I was twenty-six I married a woman named Vera who seemed in almost every way that mattered different from Marie. Vera was tall where Marie was short, was blond where Marie was dark, had a career where Marie (of course, she was only twenty-one when we married) had none. Vera also had a smaller nose and larger breasts. Both were demonstrative and affectionate before marriage and undemonstrative, relatively so, afterward. Both were intuitive and silent, liked to read or muse, valued privacy.

Vera and I stayed together for six years, a triumph of endurance over lassitude, a period in which I continued to mourn the loss of Marie. In the second year of our marriage, Vera and I had a child we named Arthur and called, for some reason that now eludes me, Bud. In the dog days of our marriage, Bud was our only common interest. He kept us busy, kept us out of each other's way, involved us in his upbringing. He was a difficult child, demanding and unsatisfied. The years have diminished his willfulness, though at a certain price.

Vera, if she wanted anything, wanted more privacy than marriage allowed. We separated at the end by mutual agreement, though not without some residual hostility, and I realized that we had spent six years of marriage hiding from each other. Just when we learned how to fight it was all over.

I didn't think I would marry again after Vera and said as much whenever the subject came up. Twice in one lifetime was sufficient, I said. The remark staled through overuse.

I saw Marie shortly after Vera and I separated, met her in the Village for lunch. What I do remember is what we ordered (Marie had a spinach salad and I had a Spanish omelet) and that neither of us had much appetite. What did we talk about? We brought each other up to date on our lives, made up stories (I speak for myself), or rearranged the past to make it a subject of more than usual interest. Marie, from her own account, had been married twice since I had spoken to her last, and was about to split up with the most recent tenant of her heart. Her third husband was in real estate and doing well, but he had become so crass and money-concerned, my former child bride could barely stand to be in the same house with him. He had not always been that way. When she married him he had been a history teacher in high school, a sensitive man tender with children, working spare hours toward a Ph.D. I told her some about Vera, as little as I could without seeming to be stingy.

In any event, Marie was less interested in my story than in her own. I talked only to occupy the spaces she left open to me. Vera and I, I said on occasion, completing the sentence in various ways. Marie laughed, slightly incredulous. It was as if she believed that no other name but hers might be coupled with mine. She was less pretty (if pretty was ever the word for what she had), had lost that astonishing glow I remembered. I felt no compelling attraction in her company. As soon as we were separated, however, the old enchantment returned and I regretted not having arranged to see her again. If I could have seen her a few more times, I might have gotten her out of my system. As it was, for weeks afterward I recalled our dialogue, embarrassed at my failure to express myself with the slightest wit or charm.

Nine months after my divorce from Vera, I moved in with a twenty-five-year-old social worker named Harriet Wilkes— that is, we moved in with each other. Part of the time we stayed at her place and part of time mine, neither of us willing to make much of a commitment. Harriet, by turns, adored and resented me, saw me as an encroachment on her need for detachment and independence. My feelings for Harriet were harder to classify. I liked her because she had a capacity for taking pleasure, seemed on superficial acquaintance almost wholly without guilt. I admired that in her, hoped to acquire some of that quality through infectious contact. Where Marie, my touchstone, was imprisoned by certain private needs, Harriet gave the impression of being emotionally unfettered. She sang in public when the mood took her, unconcerned with being thought foolish or crazy by people she didn't know.

I don't quite remember why Harriet and I broke up, but we did, I know that much, after a year and a half of relentless shuttling between our separate apartments. I remember talking to my shrink about her, and I am clearer about what I said to him than what Harriet and I said to each other at the end. I told him that I thought that Harriet was frightened of becoming too dependent and so provoked a crisis from which there was no return. "What was your part in all that?" he asked me. "I too wanted out," I said. "It was a burden living up to her idea of me. I could see that she was becoming disillusioned, and it was making me edgy."

Unless memory deceives me, Harriet and I never talked about coming apart. It was never a matter of conscious concern. At some point we started to avoid each other, to invent opportunities to be separate. Her presence began to irritate me, her odd enthusiasms, her gratuitous exhilaration. The very qualities that had attracted me to her seemed in changed light to be defects of character. One day, when I was away at work, she collected whatever she felt she had title to and moved out. I was sorry when she was gone, though not regretful enough to pursue her return.

In her absence I conceived a passion for her I had rarely felt in the time we lived together. We had one ugly fight and one passionate reunion before resigning ourselves to conclusion. Breaking up has never been easy for me.

I was thirty-three when Harriet and I came apart. It was time, I recall telling myself, for my life to take a more serious turn. I was ready to give up any and all pretense to heroism. I was in the market for a down-to-earth woman with a head on her shoulders, someone substantial and sane who would accept me and even love me as is. At the same time, I was also considering a change in career, having been stuck at the same place for too long. It had been my history to be disaffected with my immediate occupation no matter what it was. There was always something else that I was not doing that seemed more appropriate to my talents or more challenging or more lucrative. I started out wanting to paint, though gave that up early, recognized that I would never be good enough to justify the kind of commitment I would have to make. So I moved to photography and from there— one interest sliding into another—to film. Vera encouraged me, though her encouragement, I am embarrassed to report, tended to have the opposite effect of its apparent intent. I felt compelled to resist her plans for me, even when they corresponded to what I wanted for myself. I did go to film school for a while, though I found it to be, like most educational institutions, something of a fraud. They taught technique as if there were nothing else. I learned what they had to teach—even made a short film in collaboration with a friend—though lost my appetite for movies. When I left film school I took a job in advertising so as not to be dependent on Vera's support. Vera urged me to do something with filmmaking, was willing, she insisted, to be the breadwinner until I established myself. So I took a job in advertising as an art director—some still photography involved—a stopgap position I never found occasion to leave.

What I did with my life—I see that from my present vantage—was never quite the same as my intention for it. After Harriet, I believed myself ready for a serious relationship and instead became involved with two women at the same time. It was as if each were a part of some delusory ideal. Let me modify that. Either woman was sufficient, more than I deserved. Neither unfortunately was Marie, for whom the imagination trembled. Katherine was my age, a month older to the day, was separated from her husband, had a child of nine (away at school), and worked part-time as a copywriter for the company that employed me. She had had a difficult and unhappy life—a brutalized childhood, two bad marriages, the second of which ending in the disclosure that her husband preferred members of the same sex.

We had occasional lunches together, advised each other on relations with the opposite sex, offered each other consolation and comfort. Fair to say, we shared sadnesses. Katherine is and was a sad person. Her mouth seemed permanently turned down in a half circle. Her smile was a straight line; her lips would take pleasure no further. Yet she was not a sour person when we were together. She could even be quite cheerful and amusing in her dour way. I liked

118

that the face she showed me was different from the one she presented to the world.

Felice, on the other hand, was childlike, an adolescent at twenty-seven with an aversion to growing up. She was both exceptionally intelligent and astonishingly naive, a combination that charmed me to the ears. She was difficult, let it be said, sassy, willful, a person of unpredictable moods, and I was taken with her, taken by her, enthralled. Whereas I could relax with Katherine, I had to woo Felice continuously. To neglect her for a few days was to invite a disrepair that might take weeks to heal.

Felice made me feel alive, which is to say kept me in a fever of uncertainty. Since Katherine made almost no demands, I rarely thought about her when we were apart. If I had to, if Felice demanded it, I would have given up seeing Katherine. Which is what happened, which is what was bound to happen. On the other hand, I had too much invested in winning Felice to relinquish her on any terms. I admit this with self-reproach, with considerable after the fact regret. For a time, I managed to see them both as often as possible, moved between them like a gardener. That was my presumption, one which sustained me during this unsettled period in my life.

The pressure of sustaining two love affairs, or keeping news of each away from the other, kept me in a constant state of anxiety. As it turned out, I was harboring a secret that didn't exist. Both women knew of or suspected the existence of the other long before it was unequivocally in the open. And it went on after that for several months, my double life, not so much openly as tacitly. Neither woman saw fit to demand that I discard the other. The situation left me confused and mildly depressed.

Oddly, Felice seemed more hurt by the revelation than Katherine, accused me with uncharacteristic bitterness of hiding my true character from her. "It's the people that appear honest who are the most devious," she told me once, the implication inescapable. Katherine took infidelity as part of the nature of things, a fulfillment of her deepest expectations. She felt confirmed, released temporarily from the burden of her sadness. The grace of Katherine's behavior excited my admiration. It was during that period that I considered giving up Felice and committing myself to Katherine. And then Felice, without prior indication of change of heart, refused to see me. The loss felt unbearable, was like losing Marie for a second time. I became frantic and irrational, neglected my work, neglected Katherine.

I remember going to Felice's loft one lunch hour, bearing a bouquet of purple tulips, my visit unannounced. I thought the element of surprise might be to my advantage. (I find myself using the same phrase whenever I tell the story — "the element of surprise." What does it really mean?) What I dreaded more than anything else was finding another man with her. She was alone, and let me in without an argument. She said nothing at all as I remember, was willfully silent, her mouth turned downward as if wearing a mask of Katherine's face. It struck me that way at the time, the kind of perception one has in a dream. When I moved to embrace her she held me away at arm's length. "I'd like to do a sketch of you," she said. "I've never gotten you down right." I found myself seated in a narrow wooden chair, holding a pose against a predilection to do anything but sit still. She scolded me when I moved, kept me in my uncomfortable regimen for at least a half hour. When I complained she said, "I'm teaching you patience."

When I could bear no more I got up from my imprisonment to look at what she had done. There were three sketches overlaid one almost on top of the other as if the original image were sending off reverberations.

"It's not finished," she said in the cool voice she had taken on, the ice at the bottom of the fire. "Will you please go back to your chair?"

I did as I was told. After adding a few more touches, she tore the drawing in half.

"Why did you do that?" I asked, pained by her gesture.

"Half a drawing for half a relationship," she said, smiling queerly.

It's odd how you perceive people mostly in terms of your response to them. Since Felice had always had the upper hand in our relationship, I had not allowed myself to be aware of her vulnerability. That afternoon she had a tantrum in which she screamed and threw things, a side of her I had never seen before. I stood around awkwardly, dodging missiles, saying the wrong things, looking to find some way to comfort her. At some point, I shouted over her screaming that I loved her.

The tears stopped almost immediately. "If you really loved me," she said, "you wouldn't have to see that other woman."

There's something about saying flat out to someone that you love her. The words, at least in my case, tended to make their own commitment. I conceded—it was the inevitable next move—that if we were together again, I wouldn't need anyone else. Felice said she wanted time to think about what I had said, that things might have already gone too far in the wrong direction. I didn't go back to work that afternoon, and we healed our rift, discovered the pleasures of making up.

When over dinner I reported my decision to Katherine, the lines of her mouth turned further downward than I had ever seen them before. I felt awful, wanted to shout at her— the restaurant was so noisy we could barely hear ourselves talk—that I loved her, but of course I didn't. Such a gesture didn't allow itself to be repeated without falsifying its original moment. Yet who was to say that this impulse was less genuine than its predecessor?

121

Katherine took the news with exceptional dignity, shaming me all the more. When we parted, she shook my hand and said, "I wish you luck."

Even if I don't quite believe in justice, there have been times in my life when its claw has touched my throat. Shortly after my break up with Katherine, I came back from the office early one day to Felice's loft where I had been living and found her in bed with the man who had the loft upstairs. "I'll go away for an hour," I said. "When I come back I want him gone."

It was one of those things you say when you feel absolutely hopeless and need to make a show of strength. I didn't return in an hour. I went home to my own apartment, had three or four bourbons, and shed a few tears for myself. Real life, I realized, never moved me as much as a book or a movie. While on my third bourbon, I received a phone call from, of all people, Marie. She had been trying to reach me for two weeks, she said.

We met at the zoo, which was my idea. I needed witnessess, I suppose, ones that spoke a wholly different language. Marie was wearing jeans and a plaid shirt, looked more radiant than she had at our last meeting three or four years back. We met without acknowledging the other's presence, as if we had been living together in silence for years. There was a full moon in the afternoon sky, a spectral image. We walked back and forth in front of the exhibit of bears, talking about the odd presence of the moon.

"I want to have a child," she said, "but my husband doesn't-think I'm mature enough. In a few years I'll be too old."

"He doesn't want children?"

The conversation might have been last week, it has that vividness for me, though in fact, almost six years have passed.

"He thinks I'm too much of a child myself. What do you

122

think? Do you think I'd make a good mother?" She touched my arm in a maternal way as she posed this question.

"Sure," I said. "Why shouldn't you make a good mother?"

"He thinks I'm too self-involved."

I asked her if she wanted to get something to drink, beer or coffee. She didn't answer, was thinking of something else. When I asked again she said she had to split in a few minutes, an appointment that could not be avoided.

"Where do you have to go?"

"That's none of your business," she said, smiling. "That's what I tell my husband all the time."

"No wonder he doesn't want to give you a child," I said.

"Are you kidding?" she punched my arm.

"Don't hit me," I pleaded. It was as though we had shed the skin of our adult lives. I felt giddy with childhood. Marie said she was cold and asked if she could wear my jacket over her shoulders. I saw it as a form of test. The next thing, I imagined, she would ask for my shirt and pants.

Marie protested from time to time that long afternoon that she absolutely had to take off—someone unnamed expecting her—though she made no effort to part. That she didn't go generated anxiety. Why was she hanging on when she had another appointment, walking aimlessly with me in the Central Park Zoo? The unfulfilled expectation of her separation intensified despair. Stay or go, I thought of saying, though didn't. Unable to break away, I sipped at her company like a secret drinker.

We are a week or so short of the present moment, are moving headlong in that direction. I am having a discussion with my wife, a heated discussion that may well turn into something worse. We are both in bad moods, both slightly out of control.

"You've been very evasive of late," she is saying. "Are you

123

trying to create suspicion, or is there something real for me to be suspicious of? I'd like to know where I stand."

"I've nothing to say, Katherine," I say. "You either trust me or you don't."

"Well, it appears that I don't," she says, her face a mask of despondency. I sit down next to her, put my hand on her arm.

"Look, don't be so unhappy, babe."

"Go away," she whispers.

"Where do you want me to go, Katherine?"

Whatever she says it is unintelligible and I am furious at her for having to ask again.

"You heard me," she says bitterly. "I said you shouldn't have married me if you didn't love me."

I know of course what she wants to hear, and I am too angry to give her that solace. My silence corroborates her grievance. I make myself a bourbon and soda, as a form of occupation, as a transient career. I am sick with guilt.

"You're asking me to hurt you," I shout at her, "and that's not what I want. Let's get out of this, huh?"

"You usually don't need to be asked," she shouts back. Then in a more controlled voice: "I'm sorry I'm such a witch. I just want to know what's going on. I don't want to be a nagging wife."

"I've seen this woman a few times," I say. "It's not serious."

The question takes a while to emerge, is punctuated by the blowing of her nose on a balled-up Kleenex. "Are you sleeping with her?"

"No," I say too quickly, unready to make full confession.

"Is that the truth? The worse thing is, there's no way I can believe you."

"If you can't believe me, why do you ask?"

"To torment myself."

"I think so."

124

The argument ends temporarily—it is like an intermission at a dance—and I browse through the weekend television section, desperate to be entertained. There is a Yankee game I might look at, though decide against.

Katherine's sadness occupies the room and I feel plagued by it as if it were a communicable disease.

I turn on her. "Look, you're making me feel terrible," I say. It is meant as an apology and is received as nothing of the kind.

Katherine looks on the verge of tears, though I know that she will not cry. I know this because she has told me that she never cries, has not let loose so much as a tear since she was fifteen. I resent her for not crying.

I resent her for not being Marie or even Felice, for not allowing herself ever to be happy. I resent her perpetual frown, her sadness like a visiting poor relation that never leaves. I resent that she puts me in the wrong by tolerating my abuses. I resent being the villain in our marriage, though the role suits me. Poor Katherine. I wish I liked us both a little better.

I have recently received a small grant to make a movie about the children of divorced parents. If it ever gets made—one always has doubts in advance—it will be my third film. As preparation, I read whatever literature I can find on the subject, interview a number of children from broken homes, including my son Bud and Katherine's daughter, Chloe.

"What about our child?" Katherine asks.

"He's only three," I remind her, "and you and I are still together."

"That's not what I meant." She doesn't say what she does mean.

The movie opens with an enlarged shot of a family photograph—mother, father, two small daughters. We get closer and closer to the photograph until it becomes a blur of

125

forms. When the camera moves back, the father is missing from the photo, has been neatly cut away.

While the camera investigates the photograph, we hear (as voices over) the comments of various children, the voices sometimes cutting in to one another.

Boy of ten: I cried every night when my dad left, but then I kind of got used to it. You can get used to anything.

Girl of thirteen: They sent me to boarding school when things went bad. I hate them both now. I really do. I'm not going to forgive them.

Boy of seven: When my father comes to get me, my mother goes into the bathroom and locks the door. I wish I could go in there with her.

The voices play into one another, become a collage of voices, as the titles come up. CHILDREN OF DIVORCED PARENTS. The titles unfold over a lush suburban lawn (the grass as green as artificial turf). A pan of the lawn indicates that it is deserted except for a lone tricycle lying on its side. A girl of about six comes out of the house, looks around, sits down on the steps in a restive manner. Then she runs to the trike, restores it, climbs on, rides around the manicured lawn in widening circles with a kind of fierce determination.

"I like the silence," Katherine, who is viewing the film, says. "It has an eerie effect."

"This is not a finished version. I was intending to use some kind of music under the titles."

"I shouldn't have said anything," Katherine says. "I thought you meant it to be silent."

The tricycle stops, seems frozen in its place, the girl staring ahead expectantly.

"It is better without any music," I say. "I'm glad you saw that."

"I guess I would also have to see it with the music to know," she says.

126

I find her unsureness almost unbearable and have to restrain myself from making an ironic comment. The comment escapes despite my intention to withhold it.

A car drives up. The child, who was eager at its approach, turns her head away and pretends not to see it. As the man opens the door of the car, the camera moves in on his face, which is marked by a mix of expectancy and tension. We see the man pick up the child and hold her in the air. The frame freezes.

"I find this depressing," Katherine says. "Do you mind if I don't watch?" She gets up from the couch and, hunched over, quivering slightly, edges out of the room.

We cut to the inside of the house, to a woman standing by a window surreptitiously looking out. She turns away then turns back again. The camera pans the lawn from left to right, as if looking for something. There is no sign of either the man or the girl. A car passes, a different car. We observe it until it leaves the frame.

It is not quite as I visualized it in my mind—that is, the sequence merely approximates what I think of as its ideal realization.

I hear Katherine banging around in the kitchen and imagine on the flimsiest of evidence that she is taking dishes out of the dishwasher and putting them in the cupboard. She may be playing a makeshift musical instrument for all I know, one that specializes in discordant sounds. I shut off the projector.

In a few minutes I will go into the kitchen and talk to Katherine. I will tell her about Marie and about my obsession with regaining what I had lost, the entire story from the beginning. When I am ready—I am almost ready—I will go into the next room and take Katherine's hand. I will say, "There is something I need to tell you." She may not want to listen, but I will insist on telling my story. There is no point in us all being so sad.

127

THE DINNER

PARTY

I have a rule, one of few—perhaps my only rule—that I never discuss work in progress. To talk about something not fully born is to risk, as I see it, unspeakable loss. So when at a dinner party this youthful, gray-haired woman on my right, Isabelle something, some other man's discontented wife, asked me what I was working on, I hedged my answer. This is what I said. I'm working on a novel about a marriage in the process of invisible dissolution. Isabelle gave me an odd, almost censorious look and returned to the business of eating. Had I said the wrong thing? Did she think I was telling her something about her own life? I had said more than I wanted to say, though perhaps less than she felt it her right to know.

The loss of my audience so early in the proceedings seemed a depressing omen. It provoked me to want to regain her attention. It is a mistake to let yourself get challenged like that at the house of strangers.

For three consecutive nights Joshua Quartz had dreams that included the appearance of his estranged wife, Genevieve. Six months had passed since their separation, and he had considered himself free of her until the dreams presented themselves like undiscovered evidence with a significant bearing on the case. There was a progression in the dreams, as if they were installments in some larger yet undefined unit.

"Isn't there anything else you'd like to know?" I asked, trying to make a joke out of a serious question. She was chewing her food—her turkey or chicken—and couldn't find her way clear to making an answer. She held up one finger as if to say, Give me time. I waited, looked around the table and realized there was no one I knew well at this party. The Garretsons, friends of my former wife, had invited me out of some misplaced idea of kindness. For some reason, I was the only one at the table—there were fifteen guests in all—who had not yet been served. Isabelle turned to me and said, "Of course I want to know everything. Do I dare to ask?"

In the first dream, Joshua was in a small bedroom talking to a man—his father? brother? a doctor acquaintance?— about problems he was having with his back. The door to his bedroom was open, offering him a partial view of a long hallway. His wife, Genevieve, was on the phone at the furthest point of his vision. She was talking to an unnamed man, her current boyfriend, whom she referred to from time to time as darling. He felt the inappropriateness of the endearment in its present context and was more amused than pained by it. The man in his room continued to talk—something about wrapping the back in Corning's fiberglass—but his attention was on Genevieve. She turned to see if he was there, and their eyes met. She seemed to smile at him. As a matter of choice, he declined to smile back. She continued to watch him while she talked on the phone.

I felt a kick under the table and moved my leg away, thinking it an accident. The second kick suggested intention, a statement of presence from the woman on my right. I returned the kick or perhaps kicked someone else, a few heads raised from their plates, a few pained looks here

129

and there. "Consider it a down payment," said the woman, Isabelle something, putting one of her braised potatoes on my plate. "This is a novel about two people, two wary romantics, with unrealistic expectations," I said. Then I ate the potato the woman had given me. It created a desire for more, and I stared longingly at the three other potatoes on her plate. "Sometimes I just want to scream," Isabelle said. She speared one of her potatoes and held it to her lips, held it suspended in air while she considered its fate. "What you're giving me is what I could get from the dust jacket," she whispered. "Aren't you being just a little bit evasive?"

In the second dream he had come home to his new apartment to discover several radical changes in his absence. For one, the lace curtain on his door had been replaced by a white apron. He knew what it meant, knew instantly that Genevieve was somewhere in the house and that the apron was her calling card. He admired the wit of the apron, though considered its presence inappropriate in a place a man lived in by himself. He planned to take it down at first opportunity. What was going on? His cleaning woman, Henrietta, was in the kitchen preparing a turkey, stuffing it with olives and apricots. The house was pulsing with preparations for some holiday dinner. He went back to the vestibule door and removed the apron, intending to replace it with the original curtain, which was not to be found. The door looked naked without a covering, suggested deprivation and loss. He worried that Genevieve would make a fuss about his removing the apron, would take it as a rejection of her gift. When he put it back he couldn't get it straight, so he left it hanging at an awkward tilt.

Joshua washed his hands, then went to the bedroom to change his clothes, saw Genevieve in the adjoining room at his desk. Nothing is said. He starts to undress, lifting his shirt over his head. He glances at her to see if she is watching him. It is hard to tell. The book she is reading covers her face. The title, he notices, is *The Curtain Falls.*

The hostess, Kiki Garretson, served me a bowl of shell-shaped pasta in a green sauce. It was not what the others had, but was certainly an acceptable substitute. I had a reputation when younger for preferring pasta to almost anything. Perhaps the Garretsons had made this separate dinner especially for me. Or perhaps they had run out of the main course and this was a leftover from another party. "What the people in your novel love," Isabelle whispered in my ear, emphasizing each word like a radio announcer, "is the idea of being loved. Isn't that the point?"

I chewed quickly, as quickly as the pasta, which was a touch crisp, allowed, not wanting to lose this audience. Her hand was on my knee, a gentle weight. "Yes and no," I said. I looked around the table to see if anyone was watching us. "They are both married to others when they fall in love. Their relationship begins in passion and ends in anger and insentience. Ends in the death of feeling." My neighbor nodded her head in acknowledgement, confirmed in some private unhappy truth. "There's nothing worse than the death of feeling," she said, giving me the last and largest of her potatoes. We exchanged sad smiles.

The third dream was the most elaborate. He was with her in an underground parking lot, collecting their car. They were going somewhere together, the destination urgent though obscure. It was as if they were a team of some sort, detectives like Steed and Mrs. Peele or Nick and Nora Charles, a partnership that had survived other disaffections. In this case, they both knew too much. This too much knowing, this excessive knowledgability has put them in a kind of danger, a danger that offers more thrill than anxiety, a danger without menace. The fact is, they are having fun,

131

pursuing or being pursued. Affectionate wisecracks are exchanged. They get into a waiting taxi, and Genevieve says to the driver in a perfunctory voice, "Follow that car." In the next moment they are pursuing a Lincoln limousine, tearing around corners as in movie chase scenes, going through stop signs, riding on sidewalks. They hear the squeal of brakes as they flash through an intersection, but there is no sign of other cars. The canopy of a fruit stand collapses, oranges and apples roll into the street. It's just like a movie, he thinks, which is what he hears himself saying. "Who's with the children?" she asks him. "I thought you were," he says. Talk of the children deflates his exhilaration. It is too serious a topic, too rueful and painful a topic in light of their present roles. The limousine they have been following stops in front of an Italian restaurant called Pasta Mia. No one emerges from the limousine, and they wait expectantly in their cab for some further revelation.

The shells on my plate were not sufficiently cooked, crackled when chewed, though I said nothing, letting the crunching sound speak for itself, not wanting to seem ungracious. "I've been holding my breath waiting for you to continue," said my neighbor on the right. "I hope you don't mean to disappoint me." I was reluctant to continue but felt I owed her a few more details, having already taken her this far. "They can't keep apart," I said, "so hate the other for the loss of freedom and self-respect. They agree to stop seeing each other, which only intensifies irrational necessity. It goes on this way for a while, the resolution not to see each other, the breaking of the resolution, false endings, new beginnings, guilt, regret, passion, unforgivable recriminations." When I looked down I noticed another potato on my plate, smaller though more perfectly formed than either of the first two. It was gemlike, this potato, and I had not noticed it on her plate before. I ate it slowly, sensuously, holding it on my tongue for a time before swallowing it in two bites. "And what kind of credit does that get me on the literary market place?" she said.

They tell me my paralysis is a state of mind. I don't move because no matter what I say to the contrary, I don't want to move. This is not something I'm willing to believe. They carry me from bed to chair in the morning. How do I start? They bring me my food. Sometimes they — one or the other of them — feed me. Sometimes they leave the food for me on a black plastic tray, and when they're out of the room I feed myself. I can only move my arms when no one is watching. Not everything I say is true. My memory is short.

Taylor Garretson came by and filled my wine glass, asked if everything was satisfactory. My plate, I noticed, was the only one around the large table that still had food on it. "I've been talking too much," I said. I studied the food on my plate with apologetic regret, took a small forkful of the brittle shells. My companion on the right, the one who had given me her potatoes, Isabelle something, winked at me. The woman on the left, who had hardly noticed me before, turned her head in my direction. In fact, everyone at the table was looking at me with apparent curiosity. I held up my wine glass. "To a better year than the last," I said. The others joined me in the toast, all but the woman on my left, who had turned her head away.

Joshua departs the cab and enters the restaurant while his estranged wife stays behind. There is no one inside Pasta Mia that he knows or has even seen before, though they are almost all undefinably familiar. It is a family restaurant and everyone there is sitting at the same table. Joshua asks to speak to the owner. When the owner wearing a chef's apron comes out from the back, Joshua can't remember what it is he is supposed to ask. His wife comes in, takes his arm, says this is the wrong place, darling, we haven't a moment to lose. Some cliché like that. They run together for a few blocks, Genevieve glancing behind her to check on the distance of some apparent pursuer. It strikes Joshua that the owner of the Pasta Mia was the man in the limo they had been following, that the apron he was wearing had been put on as a disguise. "Who's behind us?" he asks. "Never mind," she says. Joshua is thinking that this experience with his estranged wife requires further definition. "It's been the man in the apron all along," he says, "hasn't it?" The intimacy of being pursued together touches him. Genevieve makes no comment. They arrive at their former apartment where he drops her off. "Are you going to be all right?" he asks. "Let's do this again sometime," she says. Joshua is trying to find a language for his feelings. Genevieve hesitates at the door, thinks perhaps of inviting him in. They neither embrace nor shake hands. She goes inside.

"I don't have the whole picture," Isabelle said to him. "Something crucial has been left out. I hope you're not one of those writers who leaves things out in order to be obscure." I was playing with the remainder of my shells, crushing them with my fork into a greenish powder. "Did I tell you how they met?" I asked. "I don't remember," she said. I didn't remember whether I had either. "They met in a mixed doubles game at The Wall Street Racquet Club," I said. She shook her head, pointed her finger at me. "You know that's not true," she said. I felt the detail was wrong and I wondered how I could take it back without destroying my credibility with her. "The tennis game was in an earlier draft," I said. "In a more recent version, they meet in an analyst's office. She has the appointment before him. They nod to each other for months before they begin to talk. What's important is not how they met but the intuitive sympathy

134

they felt for each other." My plate was removed with the others, and I felt a sudden gnawing hunger. "Yes?" she said.

Let me start again in a more direct and honest vein. I can stand if I have to. I can walk. I can feed myself as ably as the next person. I walk from bed to door and back again, go the whole route. Most of the time I lie in bed with my hands under my head, thinking about getting up and walking around the room. The door is locked. I am a prisoner in my own room. They bring me my meals on a black plastic tray three times a day. Perhaps the meals arrive no more than twice a day. I tend to exaggerate for effect. My memory is a string of broken connections.

"She was crying one day when he arrived late for his appointment, crying and putting on her coat with no success. Her grief moved him. He helped her with her coat. She took it as her due, thanked him without saying so. When his own session was over she was still in the waiting room." The salad course was served. The woman on my left addressed me directly for the first time. "My husband hates salad," she said. "The children, particularly the older boys, won't touch it with a pole. I think that's a shame." I smiled politely, took a forkful of leaves. "I've come to salad late myself," I confessed. "But now I can't get enough of it, particularly when it's good." "You have a good attitude for a man," she said, "but in my unsolicited opinion" — she lowered her voice — "there's more to salad than leaves."

I felt a pinch from the other side and turned toward Isabelle. "He was helping her on with her coat," she said. "They were in the waiting room of his shrink. It was the first time they had talked." The woman on the other side was also saying something, my attention divided. "He invited her for coffee," I said, then turned to the salad woman to see what she wanted.

135

Joshua called Genevieve the morning after the third dream. He didn't know what he wanted to say, let the conversation unfold to no purpose. Finally, he mentioned the dream, the first of the three. "I haven't dreamed of you at all," she said with what sounded over the phone like regret, as if she had failed to honor her part of the bargain. "I haven't even thought about you," she said, "though I like hearing your voice over the phone."

The dessert is some kind of berry cobbler — boysenberry is my guess — with a white sauce. As we are waiting to be served, Isabelle said in a somewhat plaintive voice, "What have you and Desiree been chatting about?" Desiree? "You know who I mean," she said, indicating with her eyes the woman on my left. "Nothing of consequence," I said. The salad plates were being retrieved, and it came to my attention that I had eaten only two leaves. "In their first few years together, they were obsessively jealous of one another, the woman perhaps more than the man. Because they had started out illicitly, they felt increasingly uneasy as a legitimate couple, feared betrayal." "Wait a minute," Isabelle said, "they're still in the therapist's office, they've just begun to talk, he's holding her coat for her." "If I get too specific, I'll never be able to tell you the gist of the story." "What's the matter with people?" said Isabelle, aggrieved. "Why must they ruin everything?" My neighbor on the left was saying something about leaving my salad in the lurch. "After what you told me, I was hoping you would set an example for my husband." The hostess had started to serve the cobbler when she realized she had forgotten an intervening course and so she collected the plates and returned the dessert to the kitchen. We were crestfallen as a group. The delay seemed intolerable.

The door to my room is not really locked or is only locked

from the inside when it suits me to lock it. In truth, my legs are tired. My back is bad. I have no inner life. I sleep half the day. When I leave the room, which is rare, I go directly to the kitchen to get myself something to eat. I go from my room to the kitchen and then from the kitchen directly to my room. Sometimes I walk into the closet and stand among the shirts and jackets, as if I too were something inanimate, something to put on and take off.

"He invites her for coffee after finding her in the waiting room when his own session is finished. She thinks of all the reasons she can't go or shouldn't and offers them with her apology for refusing him. They are only words, and once they are out of the way she gladly goes along. They talk for several hours, find themselves of like mind on a number of subjects. It becomes a ritual, this after-therapy assignation, and both look forward to it, both thrive on it. It is the talk that does it. They are both verbal people. Words fly between them like kisses. They are in love before they make love. And then it takes three years for them to disentangle from other relationships." I stopped for breath and Isabelle said, "You don't have to say anymore." The host and hostess, I notice, are huddled together in the doorway between kitchen and dining room, planning some new strategy. In a moment, the hostess goes back into the kitchen and returns again with cobbler. She wears an apologetic smile. "I'm not a dessert person," Desiree says to me. "I'm going to give you mine." Isabelle says something of the same. New possibilities for my story dance in my head, and I long to try them out on Isabelle, though I wait for the plates of dessert to be passed around.

I have an antique rocking chair in my room where I take comfort in moments of panic. The rocking of the chair stimulates recollections of sweeter times. I sit and rock until the circulation stops in my left leg then I get up, force myself to get up. I shake my frozen leg until it unnumbs itself. The shaking of the leg tires me. I am in the business of conserving energy, storing it up like food in wartime for a crisis even more unimaginable than the present one. If for some reason I leave the room, I am filled with uneasiness, as if the air that sustains were no longer available.

I have two plates of cobbler in front of me. The woman on my right, Desiree, has given me hers after I've already taken one for myself. When I return her dessert, Desiree refuses to accept it, slides it back toward me. "Please," she says. "It makes me happy for you to have it." Meanwhile, Isabelle has pushed her plate toward me from the other side. So: I have three plates of boysenberry cobbler with *crème anglaise* in front of me. "She doted on him in the beginning," I said to Isabelle. "It was too much. It left no place for their romance to go." "Did she?" said Isabelle in a dreamy voice. "What a coincidence." They were short a dessert on the other side of the table and I gave over one of mine, the one that had been intended for me. I still had the two gift desserts, though I wasn't sure where to start, not wanting to offend either of my companions. "If you're not going to eat it . . . " Desiree said and reclaimed her cobbler. Isabelle was chipping away at the other one with a spoon. As I took my first bite, her spoon brushed my fork. "Why didn't you keep yours if you wanted it," I asked her. "It's better than I imagined," she said, "and what's more I wanted to share it with you. If you had taken Desiree's and not mine, I would have been heartbroken." Her husband, or the man I thought was her husband, was watching us from the other side of the table.

I walk a block from the house after breakfast and then, as if invisible chains pull me back, return to my room. In the street, sometimes I pass a woman walking a small terrier, and we nod to each other. Sometimes she makes a comment on the weather, an innocuous, impersonal comment. Like: Not so cold today, is it? I share her pleasure in the weather's improvement. I think of things to say to her, variations on our usual exchange. I work up conversation in my hermetic room, rehearse it in the mirror before going out. This is what I will say to her.

There is, as it turns out, another course brought belatedly, out of traditional sequence, to the table. A broccoli soufflé with a plum glaze. "This is Bozo's dish," the hostess says. (Taylor's nickname is Bozo.) Taylor stands, bows, shakes a fist in triumph. Desiree whispers: "He's a terrible cook, you can't imagine." I am the only one at table who eats Taylor's dish. Except for the fact some of the broccoli is still frozen, it is not so bad, not as bad as advertised. Desiree, I notice, has covered her plate with her napkin, apparently unable to bear even the sight of the dish. I said to Isabelle, "In the beginning they talked like angels to each other. After they made love, there seemed nothing else to say." "It makes me sad to think about it," Isabelle said.

There is a cheese course next, followed by coffee, followed by glasses of some green liqueur. During all this, Isabelle and I hold hands under the table. From time to time, I feel compelled to throw out morsels of my novel in her direction, whatever comes to mind. I am aware that the party will be over soon, that someone will get up to leave, and that the others will follow. An intense sadness overwhelms me.

Genevieve called Joshua in the middle of the night, waking him from a restive sleep. "I want to tell you that I've been dreaming about you," she said, "Look, I'm sleeping," said Joshua. "Why can't you call in the morning like any sane person?"

139

"My dream," she said, "concerned a dinner party at our old house on Watkins Place." She laughed to herself. "Everyone around the table was naked. You were the only one with clothes on, the only one. I was disappointed in you at first. I thought, how gauche to stand out like that, to not get in to the spirit of things. Then I thought, what terrific integrity. You retained your dignity, your propriety, while others had yielded to some pointless fashion."

Joshua thanked her for the compliment.

"That's not the end," she said. "I went upstairs to get dressed to show the others that I was on your side in this. When I got back to the dining room, you had gone off with someone else."

"I hate to say good-by to people I like," Isabelle said. "Someday you'll have to tell me how your novel ends. Perhaps I'll see it in the window of a bookstore and go in and buy a copy."

"I told you all I know," I said. "At this point, you know about as much as I do."

"I don't believe that," she said. "How can you possibly say something like that? I think you've been trying to pique my interest. Yes?"

I had nothing to deny. The telling had neglected the structure, of course, the formal concerns, the flashes of language, the urgency of experience. The transitions. What had been left out, when I thought of it, was everything. The rest had been devalued by recitation, had slipped away into the smoke.

I held her coat for her. "The next time I see you, I'll have more to tell," I said. We shook hands in a businesslike manner.

"Until then," she said, following her husband out the door and into the night.

140

PASSION?

A man I know, a longtime sometime friend, recently left his wife and three children because he had fallen in love with another woman. Such news has a disquieting effect on our crowd. Henry is the most domesticated and repressed husband among us, the most devoted of fathers. If Henry, our moral light, is capable of such anarchic behavior, it strikes us that almost anything is possible. Surmise, however, is not the business of this report. What I mean to do here is to separate the knowable evidence from unwarranted conjecture. I mean to investigate the mystery of Henry's inexplicable act as though I were a detective tracking down a criminal.

2

Henry was barely twenty-four when he married Illana. They had met at college, had started going together when Henry, who was a year or so older, was in his sophomore year, though they had known each other casually (or such is the story one pieces together) from childhood. There were times, says Illana, when each was the other's only real friend. Her remark is not surprising. Henry and Illana had always seemed, to those of us who thought we knew them well, exceptionally close. They had grown over the years of their marriage to seem like mirror images of one another. One breathed in, we supposed, and the other breathed out. They saw themselves, and we tended to confirm that view, as a perfect couple.

3

The year before he married Illana, Henry, then a Rhodes scholar, started work on a novel about a young intellectual affianced to his childhood sweetheart who falls in love during a summer abroad with a French woman twelve years his senior. He wrote 126 pages of this book before giving up, and the manuscript apparently still exists in its first and only draft. It was, insofar as anyone knows, Henry's only attempt at prolonged fiction.

4

In the second year of their marriage, their first daughter, Natalia, was born. Henry and Illana were extremely serious about the responsibility. Shortly after that, Henry, an up-and-coming editor, moved to a job in another publishing house that paid twenty dollars more a month. Illana also was working, and they had a live-in maid to look after the child. Henry announced, we all remember, that Illana's working was a temporary arrangement, that it was the preference of both of them that she stay home with the child. Illana said that she and Henry on that matter were in thorough agreement. She made this assertion, as I remember, with surprising passion.

5

Henry was under a great deal of pressure at work and went into therapy to avoid, as he said, breaking down altogether. He had a dream—his therapist had been after him to write down his dreams—in which his father, whom he hadn't seen in ten years, came to him and said that there was evidence that someone was shooting at him, and he won-

142

dered if it were Henry. Henry said that he admitted to being angry at his father for having walked out on his mother, but that he had no recollection of trying to kill him. The father said if thoughts could kill, Henry would have to be number one suspect. Thoughts don't kill, said Henry. Well, how do you explain the bullet in my stomach? said the father.

6

About that time Henry reported to friends that he and Illana were reading to each other in bed at night. "We are going through the entire canon of Dickens," said Illana, "one chapter a night." "How long will it take to do all the novels?" someone asked. Henry, figuring to himself, a private smile on his face, said nothing. "We'll do it until we decide not to do it," said Illana.

7

Illana had written a children's book in her spare time. Henry agented it for her, showing it to children's book editors at two other publishing houses, avoiding his own as a matter of moral discretion. Illana and Henry had always taken impeccable moral positions. And though they didn't presume to judge others, one sensed a certain discomfort with the unscrupulous or overweaningly ambitious. Illana withdrew the book at some point, indicating that she had no great desire to make her work public.

8

I spoke to Henry at the hospital after the birth of his second daughter, Nara. He said, although he and Illana had wanted a boy, they were not in any way disappointed. Illana said the same thing to my wife in almost the same language, impressing on us (was it meant to?) how together they were, how intimately allied. A week later, when we visited them at home, Henry in Illana's presence made the same speech. When we got home my wife said, "Perhaps they protest too much," and I said, no, I thought they meant it. "It's the same thing," she said.

9

We all admired the seeming ease with which Henry rose in his chosen profession. What was most impressive was that his ambition, which evidence suggests was considerable, was never agressively displayed. He had never, not to our knowledge at least, advanced his career at the expense of someone else. We had almost never heard a bad word of him. Yet at the same time, we felt that Henry's full capacities were not being realized. What we meant by that was not at all clear.

10

What do we know about Illana? When friends of Henry's and Illana's get together, the question tends to come up. What has she had to say for herself in all the years we've known her? We thought of her as taciturn, though not unfriendly, a bit formal in manner, a woman who spoke her opinions as if they were national secrets. She had a way of looking after her children—this was when Henry was there to help—without making it seem, as do some mothers, that the job was overburdening her. We can enumerate her qualities with no strong sense of knowing the person who contains them.

11

This is Henry's story mostly. It is Henry who announces one day, while Illana sits at the kitchen table with the baby on her lap, that he has fallen in love with someone else. "You have?" Illana is imagined to have asked. "What does that mean in terms of our marriage?"

"I don't know," said Henry. "It's too new to me."

"You don't know?" The question asked with some manner of skepticism. "What do you want to do?"

"What do you want me to do?"

"Well, naturally," Illana said softly, "I'd like you to break it off if you can."

"Out of the question," said Henry.

"I didn't realize that it . . ." said Illana, a small crack of panic in her usually impassive face, swallowing her words as though ashamed of their inadequacy.

"It happened," said Henry. "I didn't mean it to, but it did. I'm terribly sorry."

12

After that first confession, Illana becomes a tacit partner, an accessory after the fact, in Henry's double life. Henry works out a regimen, accommodating both worlds. He has dinner with Illana and the children, helps put the children to bed, leaves afterwards to spend the night with Patricia, returning by taxi at 5 A.M. to be present when the children awake. It is important to him to have the children perceive their world as intact. (Also important perhaps to keep up appearances in front of himself and Illana, a way of deflecting awareness.) "I want you to do what's best for you," Illana is reported to have said to Henry. "I don't want to leave you and the children," said Henry, "and I can't give up Patricia." If this assertion wounds Illana, there is no visible evidence for it. After breakfast, Henry takes the oldest daughter, Natalia, to school, as he has always done, before going off himself to work.

13

The vice president of the government foundation at which Henry worked had been having an affair with the wife of one of the board of directors, and word of it—one wondered why the news had taken so long—finally reached that lady's husband. Scandal ensued and the notorious editor had no choice but to resign in favor of a slightly higher paying job at a rival house, leaving in his wake a vacancy at the top. It was rumored that Henry was in favored consideration for the post. Who knows where such rumors start? Henry, at the time, was the youngest and ablest associate director at the foundation, and it was more than possible that his well-wishers, wanting the rumor so, presumed its likelihood. Henry, taking nothing for granted, went to see the president of the foundation to indicate his interest and availability. Whatever Henry's boss said to him—the account given to me was notably short on specifics—Henry appeared hopeful in his guarded way. "Frankly," he said, "I have no reason to expect anything."

14

Illana said, out of Henry's hearing, that she thought Henry was setting himself up for a fall. "You think he won't get the job?" asked her confidante, who in this case was my wife Genevieve. "I think his chances are not as good as he thinks they are," said Illana, according to my source. It was the first any of us had heard Illana express an opinion at sharp variance to Henry's. "Of course, he deserves the job," she added. "I just don't think he's in line for it." Something odd was going on between them, we thought. Why hadn't Illana, who was the epitome of loyalty, offered this perception to Henry?

15

One day my wife asked me if I found Illana sexy? Sexy may not be the word she had used. "Attractive" or "beautiful" is more likely. I don't remember what I answered. "Uhnrr," perhaps. Something that cancelled itself out, I suspect. What's that about? I thought, though let it slide by at the time. About a week later, something else bothering me, I asked her why she had asked about Illana. "Oh," she said, "someone else was saying, I don't remember who, that Illana was the most beautiful woman of his acquaintance and I wondered if you thought the same thing." I said I didn't even think Henry thought that. "That's an odd thing to say," she said. "Well, she's beautiful in a conventional way," I said, "but there's something glacial about her as if she weren't quite alive."

16

Why do I remember my wife's question about Illana and my answer, and what do they have to do with the larger questions under investigation in this study? I think that we both felt that there was something invisibly wrong with Henry and Illana's perfect marriage, though we were not in touch with that perception. And why should we have been? Why should we have thought of Henry and Illana at all? I ask the questions merely to ask them. Illana was not the issue of my wife's question as it turned out, merely the displaced occasion. I had heard the question she had asked, but not the unspoken confession it contained.

Two days after Henry's son was born, he got word that the job he had coveted, had come in fact to count on, had been given to someone else. The news arrived, as it tends to in Henry's profession, by way of rumor, and Henry, as angry as he ever remembers himself, went to see his boss to check it out. "Don," Henry said, "I've heard some disturbing news." Don took his glasses off to listen, lit a cigarette, though he had given up smoking a week ago this day. "Well, what have you heard?" he asked. (His tone suggested, Henry reported, that there wasn't any rumor around he wasn't prepared to deny.) "I had heard," said Henry, "that you had made a decision on Calvin's replacement." "Oh that," said Don. "You said you would let me know as soon as you came to a decision," said Henry. "Did I say that?" said Don. "Frankly, I don't remember making any such promise. The feeling was, and as you know I queried opinions from all directions, that you could have done the job adequately—no one had anything negative to say about your capabilities—but that . . ." Henry had no recollection of how the sentence was completed.

18

Henry, it was reported took his disappointment with extraordinary grace, which was our idea of Henry. "That's the way it goes," he said, defending the qualifications of the man chosen in his place. "What I have to do is reevaluate my commitment to my job." Illana seemed emotionally drained. We perceived it as a form of loyalty to Henry and admired them both—this special couple—all the more.

19

The following account has been confirmed by two sources and so it is included here despite my own tendency to disbelieve it. The time was about four weeks after Henry had learned that he had been passed over for the promotion he had anticipated. The affair with Patricia, if it had already started, was some two months shy of becoming public news. Henry and Illana were at a party hosted by Henry's employer. It was a cocktail party held in some east side apartment to honor the grant recipients of that year and the living room was crowded to the walls with the mostly uninvited. Some bearded middle-aged composer, congenitally sour, took it into his head to assail Henry over the granting policy of the foundation that had just passed Henry over for promotion. Henry was polite at first, said he was not responsible for the choices of committees on which he hadn't served, then proceeded, which is typical of Henry, to defend the foundation's policies unequivocally. The composer kept after him, finding fault with one choice after another. When he could take no more—one can imagine the complication of his feelings—Henry turned his back on him. Illana, who happened to be on the periphery of the small group listening in, was heard to whisper to Henry, "Why didn't you answer him?" Henry, usually under control, lost his temper and shouted at her, "Why didn't I answer him? Why didn't I? I didn't answer him because the son of a bitch is not listening to anything I say." It is reported that Illana's face reddened and that she apologized to Henry's adversary for her husband's behavior.

20

Even after Henry moves in with Patricia, Illana continues to pretend to the children that she and Henry are together as before. "Why are you doing it?" my wife says to her when she comes to visit with the three children, who range in age from six months to six years. "If I were you, I'd tell him to fuck off." Illana, who rarely smiles, smiles at that. "I would if I felt that way," she says. "I'm not angry at Henry. I want him to be happy, and if he's happy this way, then that's the way it has to be." When Illana is gone my wife says to me: "One of these days she's going to realize how angry she really is. And then. . . ."

21

A call from Henry this morning at work. He wants us, he says, to be the first of his friends to meet Patricia. An appointment is made for dinner at a Chinese restaurant called Hunan Feast. My wife says, when she hears of the arrangement, that she won't go, that it is a disloyalty to Illana even to meet Patricia. I mention that Henry is also a friend and that there is no reason why we have to take sides. "I can't forgive him," she says, "He may be a friend of yours, but he's no friend of mine."

Patricia seems as nervous to meet us as we are to meet her, and the experience reminds me of the blind dates of my adolescence. None of us seems able to strike the right note. "What do you think?" Henry whispers out of earshot of the women. "I think she's . . . (I search for the word) fine," I say generously. My answer seems to disappoint him. "Is that all?" he asks.

22

"What do you think of her?" my wife asks when we're in bed that night, the first either of us has risked the subject. "She's different from what I imagined," I hear myself saying.

"I don't know what you mean by that." A note of irritation in her tone.

"Does that mean you don't like her?" I ask.

"It's not a question of liking or disliking her. She's nothing. She's a blank. Didn't you see that?"

150

My silence offers denial.

"My God, Joshua, I've never seen anyone with less personality. She's pathetic."

"Well, what do you think she has for Henry?"

"I haven't the faintest idea. What do you think?"

"Well, she's not unattractive," I say.

"Not unattractive? She's the most ordinary looking woman I've ever seen in my life."

23

Henry is on one of his periodic diets; we go to a health food restaurant for lunch and have a couple of shredded carrot sandwiches. Our conversation is correspondingly low on calories. "Patsy liked you and Genevieve," he says a few times, rephrasing the remark so as not to seem to repeat himself. "She felt the two of you accepted her." "She seemed extremely nice," I say. "Very . . ." The word eludes me. "Lively," he says. "Lively," I repeat. "In that way, she's the opposite of Illana," he says. "Do you think you'll stay with her?" I ask. He becomes thoughtful, which is a form of reprimand with Henry, an indication that you've overstepped yourself. Then he says with a forgiving smile: "We take every day as it comes." It goes like that until later in the meal when Henry says, "Illana and I still love each other. The situation hasn't changed that."

"Then you are thinking of going back to her?"

"It's impossible," he says, smiling enigmatically. "We're both happier this way."

"Both of you?" My incredulousness seems to escape notice.

Henry eats his yogurt and nuts with a beatific smile.

"Is it sex?" I ask, expecting no answer.

"Never been so good," he says.

"It's not sex," says my wife. We are still trying to understand our friend Henry. "Or sex is merely an excuse for something else."

"If Henry says their sex is good, why should you doubt him?"

"Henry," says Genevieve, "is trying something out. He wants to see how far he can go, how outrageous he can be, before Illana will say no more."

"That leaves out the implication of Patsy altogether," I say.

"Patsy doesn't count. Don't you see that?"

"If you ask Henry, Patsy is the only one who counts."

Our conflicting views of the reality abrade against one another, strain the limits of our friendship.

"Why are we fighting over Henry and Illana?" my wife asks.

The continuing argument becomes its own answer.

25

Henry and Patricia have been living together for six months. Henry visits with the children on weekends and sometimes comes over in the evenings to put them to bed. Illana, although she sees other men, appears to work at it as if a recommended though pointless exercise, remains in her heart faithful to the Arrangement. How do I know this? Illana tells us or tells Genevieve, which comes to the same thing. Genevieve becomes increasingly impatient with Illana's stance, though talks to her almost every day on the phone, gauging her emotional temperature from the evidence of the unspoken. "She has no idea how angry she really is," says Genevieve. "Her calm is a form of self-oblivion. Meanwhile she won't allow herself to get interested in any of the men she sees. I can't stand it."

26

My wife says, apropos of my arm around her, "You're behaving like Henry."

"What does that mean?"

"Henry and Patsy, as you know, behave like teenagers in public, but they have an excuse. They're new to each other."

Her rebuke turns into a fight. I recall my arm and take refuge in another room.

She follows after a moment. "Don't you see what you're doing?" she asks. "You're jealous that Henry has another woman."

"Maybe I am," I say.

27

I overhear Genevieve complain to Illana on the phone about me, her way, I think, of criticizing Henry indirectly. All of our men are unreliable, says her tone. And what have I done? Whatever it is, she refuses to forgive me. "I am not Henry," I say to her.

"You wish you were," she says.

I call Henry from work, but he is not available for lunch that day, which is too bad. He is precisely the person I need to talk to in my present mood. An odd coincidence: I run into Illana at lunch; she is with another man, I am with another woman. We hail each other across the restaurant. At first I didn't recognize her—how absolutely smashing she looks!—was staring at her in admiration. "We'll have to talk some time," I say to her. She says, "Yes, yes."

28

Have I drifted from the subject of this investigation? The subject itself drifts. To tell someone's story is to identify, to some extent, with the inner life of that person. In explaining Henry, I explain myself; in explaining myself, I explain Henry. Although not influenced by Henry's behavior—I am convinced that he is not my example—I have just split with my wife of ten years. My situation differs from Henry's in certain definitive ways. I haven't (at the time, at *this* time) fallen in love with anyone else. Genevieve and I weren't getting along, were fighting too much, were making each other unhappy. I realize this sounds evasive, but the disrepair of our marriage is too immediate for me to see it with any clarifying distance. It is easier, if not altogether more edifying, to talk about Henry and Illana. Henry continues to live joyfully, passionately, with Patsy, who is neither more nor less beautiful than his wife and who, despite apparent differences, resembles her more than not. Illana continues to make do and to accept her husband's manifest disaffection with public and private grace. I envy them both. My situation is neither pleasurable in itself nor might engender the admiration of others.

29

Tonight I have dinner with Illana and the two older children, sitting at the table with them in their makeshift living/dining room as I had times before in significantly different circumstances. Illana prefers, she says (the evening's arrangement is her idea), to eat with the children like a family. After dinner, I help her put them to bed, a chore of some complication. "How do you manage by yourself?" I ask. "Henry usually comes by to help," she says. "But since you were coming, I told him there was no need for him to bother." I indicate some surprise that she had mentioned it to Henry. "We have no secrets from each other," she says with that seriousness characteristic of them both.

"What now?" she asks.

The question is not meant to be answered. We sit on the sofa, holding hands, talking about nothing. At one point, she says—we have just kissed somewhat awkwardly—"Joshua, do you think of me as a cold person?" I reserve answer, kissing her again as if that urgent gesture (is it really as urgent as it seems?) were a response to her question. And yet what I think one moment ceases to be true the next. She is passionate yet remote, as if her passion were a private wellspring separate from her day-to-day nature.

30

I return to my hotel room at four in the morning and have barely dropped off when the phone rings. "I want you back," the voice says. It is odd that I am unable to identify or rather confuse the identity of that voice. I finesse my confusion. "At this moment?" I ask. "As soon as you can," says the voice. (I will know in a minute who it is, I think. Keep her talking and she will reveal herself.) "Why do you want me back?" "Oh, God! Do you have to ask? If you don't come to me, I'll come to you." She hangs up abruptly though soundlessly, fitting the phone like a piece of a puzzle into the base. Three hours later (all time is an estimate here), a knock on the door wakes me from an erotic dream. "Who's there?" I ask the nurse in my dream. The knock repeats, replays itself. I put on a bathrobe and stagger to the door, bumping invisible furniture en route. "Do you mind my coming to your room?" she asks, stepping in, locking the door behind her. Perhaps she says nothing at all, and the voice I quote is out of the interrupted dream. There is no time for questions and explanations; there is barely even time to kiss. Coupling is impersonal and urgent like some natural disaster. "Who's with the children," I ask later.

"Never mind," she says. "The children are well looked after."

31

Henry seems unusually jaunty when we meet after work at O'Neill's for a drink. I am not eager to talk to him, would have avoided this meeting if I hadn't felt obliged to face him. It takes him two drinks to get to what's on his mind. "I don't know that I like what's going on between you and Illana," he says casually and then again with added weight as if he hadn't heard himself the first time. "I've always liked Illana," I say. He nods. "She's a terrific person, and I don't want to see her hurt." Although expecting something like this— Henry is one of the most consciously moral people I know— I can think of nothing useful to say. "Are you in love with her?" he asks. "Henry, come on," I say. His face clenches and for a moment, just for a moment, he is so pissed off he can barely keep himself together. "I feel very close to Illana," he says softly. "I appreciate that," I say. His glass overturns, and the bartender comes over to mop the counter. "It's all right," he says. "I'm not angry with you." The conversation seems to repeat itself. "I don't understand what you're asking," I hear myself say perhaps for the third time. "I don't want to see Illana hurt, that's all," Henry says once again.

"Are you asking me to stop seeing her?"

"I don't think I have the right to ask you that," he says.

32

Illana seems to call at least once a day, which is all right, though sometimes I wish it were Genevieve, who never calls. One night at her place, she says, "I really want a husband, not a lover."

"You have both," I say.

"I have neither," she says. "Joshua, I'm opposed to disorder."

"I'm not sure it's over with Genevieve," I say.

Illana laughs. "She says it's over. We talk about you on the phone."

That night after the children are in bed and we have made love with our customary hunger, rushing through the act as if it might be taken from us if we waited, I have an odd perception. "You would take Henry back, wouldn't you, if he was ready to come back?"

She thinks about it and thinks about it. "I would," she says finally, "but afterward I'd be sorry."

THE LIFE

AND TIMES

OF MAJOR

FICTION

It wasn't that he was a great reader as a child but that he hardly read anything, hardly even cracked a book until he was in his mid-twenties. At least that's the story he told me. He told other people other stories, which is their business and only of peripheral concern in this report. Once he discovered books, he told me in one of his side-of-the-mouth confidences, he couldn't get enough of them. "It was like," Ernie has been quoted in print as saying, "coming of age in Samoa," though in fact he was stationed in Japan at the time, a supply sergeant in Special Services during the last months of the Korean War. Once he discovered books he wondered where they had been all his life and why no one had ever told him how astonishing they were. It was as if it were some kind of unspoken secret, he said, and those on the inside weren't generous enough to share it with those on the out. Ernie took it on himself to spread the word in a way that would make people pay attention.

2

"He was a real-life Gatsby," my friend Jack said about Ernie, "except that it wasn't a woman that inspired him to reinvent himself but a literary ideal he only partially understood." Ernie read voraciously, read everything that came into his hands, yet we wondered, we couldn't help but wonder—he was always there talking about who to read, who we *had* to read—when he found the time. There was something of the con man about Ernie, but we trusted that it was mostly an act, a facade under which sincerity and sensitivity kept unannounced watch.

3

The first fan letter he wrote, the first time he put his feelings about a book down on paper, he was embarrassed to have the author, whom he admired beyond words, read his "pathetic attempt at appreciation." Despite such misgivings, he posted the letter. "That took real guts," Ernie confided. "I thought, let the guy think I'm some kind of unwashed schmuck. I loved the man's books, and I was going to tell him regardless of the impression it made." Jack told me that Ernie sent fan letters to two writers at the same time, commending each as the most important influence in his life. Neither writer answered him, not at first, and the silence on the other end, which was how he experienced no answer, saddened Ernie. He would have answered gratefully, he told us, if someone like himself had written an admiring letter to him.

4

Then there's the story, which only some of us credit, of how Ernie, when in the service, had an extended affair with an English nurse. They were wild about each other, we heard, but various obstacles—the war not the least of them—kept them apart, intensifying the romantic aura of their feelings. Finally, tenacity was rewarded, and they lived together in idyllic circumstances for several months. The woman was pregnant with Ernie's child and Ernie was overjoyed at the prospect of being a father and spending a life with this woman. Then something terrible happened, the kind of thing that warns you against exhilaration. There were unforseen complications in the delivery. Neither mother nor child survived the birth. The news devastated Ernie, though he made no complaint, walked around in the rain as if he were composed of a thousand fragments held together by lacings of glue.

5

He wrote a second and third time to one of the writers, a recluse who hadn't published a book in eight years, and the third letter elicited a two-line response. It was typed like a ransom note.

IF MY BOOKS PLEASE YOU, FINE.
IF THEY DON'T, THAT'S ALSO FINE.

The signature was illegible, or almost illegible, but there was no question whose fine literary hand it was.

Ernie put the letter behind a plastic sheet in a photograph album, though he was unaware at the time that it was the beginning of a collection. Ernie wrote letters of admiration to other writers and began to accumulate over a period of months a handful of answers. When he got a letter from one of his writers—he couldn't help but think of them as his—it brought tears to his eyes. If he admitted it to anyone, he said, admitting it to everyone, he'd become a laughing stock. So please don't tell anyone, he told us all.

6

For a while he lived with a woman who had been a writer, who had in fact published two novels in the distant past, though had written nothing for several years, had reached a point where she could barely get a sentence down on paper she might be willing to acknowledge. "Just think what you're denying the world," Ernie would say to her, closing her in a room with a typewriter for four hours a day. Her name was Zoe. He called her Zo Zo, which occasionally sounded like So So.

Sometimes she would complete a sentence in her four hours of exile, sometimes a half page of x's, an unseen text buried beneath.

Ernie bullied her and shouted at her, but she seemed not to mind, laughed good-naturedly at his excesses.

One day she came out of her prison with a completed story, a vindication or Ernie's regimen for her. He read the story with unqualified admiration, although he had (truth to tell) some minor reservations about the ending. She said she would change a line or two if it would make him happy. "I'm happy with things as they are," he reported himself saying. "It's the opinion of posterity I'm concerned about."

7

Another time Ernie fell in love with a woman whom he used to see every morning on Broadway walking her dog. Ernie tended to walk along with the two of them, paying the dog attention, which ingratiated him with the woman. They had a brief affair, then broke up when it got serious—the woman dependent on her husband in childish ways—then came together again. Their time together was mostly disappointing, informed as it was by regret and the prospect of impending separation. They consoled themselves with the illusion that one day they would live together as an acknowledged couple. It was one of those relationships that never ended, that continued to beguile itself with hope, though Ernie and the woman saw each other less and less. And then not at all. There was a rumor that the woman threw herself under a train or took an overdose of pills, though I suspect it was untrue, had grown out of a wish to give the story a more conclusive ending.

8

It was hard to keep track of the jobs Ernie held before his rise to celebrity. In a sense certainly, they were all the same job. He started out selling aluminum siding at carnivals, then after a brief stint as a radio actor, he emerged as a book traveler for a textbook firm in Boston, which kept him away from home somewhat more than he liked. He worried, from all accounts, that Zoe would leave her room in his absence to talk on the telephone or to smuggle food from the refrigerator, temptations difficult for her to resist. Once seduced from her task, she might never return to it.

What he liked about the job was that it provided occasion to meet some of the writers whose books he admired. Beyond a few obligatory visits to the colleges in his terrain, he could use his time as it pleased him. As a matter of discretion he only looked up those writers who had answered his correspondence. He didn't court rejection, he told us, but on the other hand, he didn't let it get him down, never thought of it as personal.

9

After a whirlwind visit to the University of Maine — "I'm in and out," Ernie liked to say — he decided to look up Jason Honeycutt, who lived somewhere on the border between rural Maine and New Hampshire. The reclusive novelist had no phone, so Ernie waited for him outside the Deerfield general store, where Honeycutt, so said an informer at the university, did his shopping every Friday.

Ernie has told this story differently to different people, but I've pieced together the following account.

Ernie introduced himself to Honeycutt when the man came out of the store, offered to help him carry his groceries, which seemed to overburden the writer. Honeycutt mumbled something unintelligible and walked off to his oversized station wagon.

"I know what your privacy means to you," Ernie shouted after him. "I have no intention of imposing on you."

10

"Your books are very special to me," Ernie said. They were standing in front of Honeycutt's sprawling farmhouse, a box of groceries on the ground between them. "I just want to say that a single line of yours moves me more than the collected works of just about anyone else."

Honeycutt took a deep breath, a sigh of impatience or resignation. "All right, what are you after?" he asked.

Ernie came away from that visit with Honeycutt's avowed friendship and a signed first edition of one of the early novels. Given Honeycutt's reputation for turning away intruders, Ernie's success is all the more mystifying and impressive. The joke was, and Ernie told it on himself, that Honeycutt had bought his departure with that gift. Which didn't explain the literary correspondence that followed and Honeycutt's professed admiration, in several of his letters, for Ernie's understanding of his work.

After Ernie had won over the legendary Honeycutt, the other writers he pursued seemed to fall in line. After a point, it became a symbol of achievement to receive a letter from Ernie Sommer. Almost no writer of any distinction was ignored by him.

"They were very generous to me," Ernie has been quoted as saying. "I might have been the literary equivalent of a mass murderer for all any of them knew."

11

Ernie was extremely attached to his mother, I'm told. His father did some kind of physical labor, which seemed to use him up, shuck him of all vitality and hope. The rare occasions he spent with the family, he was often drunk and sometimes violent. Disappointed with her husband, Ernie's mother, who was artistic, turned to Ernie for consolation. Ernie took sustenance from his mother, became dependent on her affection and approval. He showed some talent for painting as a child—it was his mother's idea for him—but then he gave it up. At some point, he realized that he had to get away from his mother to survive. As he got older, he took on something of his father's manner, some of the gruffness and swagger, though he remained, even after her death, essentially his mother's son.

12

When Ernie became a literary editor—eventually he started his own publishing company, Cervantes & Sons—he took his writers with him in surprising numbers. By this time Ernie was almost as well known (his picture on the cover of *People* magazine) as the most celebrated of his writers. Ernie made light of his success, liked to say it was a case of "importance by association." "The other guys wrote these books and all I had to do was get the word around." Ernie's authors didn't tour the provinces promoting their books. He saw the practice as demeaning to serious artists so he went himself, stood in for his authors on talk shows, made public appearances at bookstores, seemed everywhere at once, developed a reputation for saying the most provocative thing that came to mind. That was when he was starting out as a publisher, the first two or three years. In the third year of his publishing venture—things came apart after that—his writers were as dedicated to him as he had been (and maybe still was, though it was no longer easy to tell) to them.

13

What went wrong? When a group of Ernie's writers get together at one of the traditional watering spots that question invariably comes up. The answers tend to be provisional and dogmatic. The favored position is that the culture tends to destroy its heroes to make room for new ones. The rival position, which had almost equal claim, is that Ernie self-destructed. The more celebrated he became the more outrageous he got. He took to referring to the audience—the first time in a radio interview in Las Vegas—as "those unwashed illiterate peckerheads out there." That didn't ingratiate him a whole lot, I suspect, or maybe it did until his listeners realized the "peckerheads" he was talking about were themselves. According to Jack, Ernie destroyed himself by trying to educate an audience that was wholly content being insulted.

14

Despite the critical success of the books Cervantes & Sons produced, the company, owned in partnership with two traditional types, managed to lose money or make so little, given the favorable attention it attracted, that it seemed like loss. Ernie was advised by his partners to practice greater economy, particularly in regard to his authors. Ernie's answer, he had told us each separately in private unrepeatable confidence, was that he practiced all the time though never seemed to get it right. One of his partners told me that after the first six months or so Ernie lost interest in the running of the firm. "He was more concerned with his own celebrity," the man told me, "than with the nuts and bolts of the business." On the other hand, Ernie had equally harsh things to say about his partners, whom he took to calling Heckyl and Jeckyl. Heckyl, he said, couldn't read and Jeckyl could but didn't.

15

We backtrack a bit here. Ernie is still on the rise, an ascending star in the lit celeb firmament. A collection of his correspondence called *Heroes and Heroines* is about to be published. As soon as he signs the contract for the book, Ernie regrets having made "my private obsession public." He insists that the book is incomplete and initiates new correspondence with a variety of international figures, forestalls publication date, dreams a letter from Tolstoy that he publishes in an obscure literary quarterly. Ernie denies that he is himself a writer. He is a longstanding appreciator of writers, an avaricious reader who is serious about what he reads, and perhaps (evidence the Tolstoy letter) a medium for literary voices. "Do you mean to say," the interviewer asks him, "that you didn't actually write the letter from Tolstoy?" "What can I tell you?" Ernie says. "I've never written anything, have never shown the slightest talent for writing. You could look it up. The 'C' I got in freshman English at the University of Pennsylvania was a generosity from the instructor. Tell you the truth, I don't know how the Tolstoy letter was written. It came to me in a moment of pure light. I think it would be ungracious of me to question the source."

A letter from Sophocles followed, though was never released for publication. Ernie himself questioned its legitimacy. "The man dictated it," he said, "but to tell the truth most of it was Greek to me."

Ernie was so self-important, one of his partners complained to me, that he would scotch film deals by abusing the person who wanted to buy the rights to one of his properties. He reputedly asked for a written critique from an independent producer who was after Jack's absurdist novel about Auschwitz. The man said that what interested him most about the novel was its wellspring of humanity. Ernie, according to the partner, told the man not to come back until he read the book word for word and had some idea what he was buying.

Whether Ernie was subversive of his own business is a moot issue. Ernie said not to believe it, that he only interfered when negotiations became wearisomely protracted. Besides, he added, he thought it immoral to sell the books he loved as if they were underarm deodorants.

Whatever the case, Ernie's partners offered to buy him out by paying him, according to the partner I interviewed, twice what his share in the firm was worth. Eight months after Ernie left, the company, in order to survive, sold itself to a conglomerate and both surviving partners, in due course, were forced out of the business.

17

Ernie had a friend, a psychologist, who ran an experimental clinic which took on only patients that had been previously diagnosed as incurable. One of the friend's incurable cases was a beautiful schizophrenic seventeen-year-old girl, who had had real or imagined relations with her father when she was twelve. When Ernie visited the friend at his clinic in California, he was moved by the girl's intelligence and courage and spent some time talking to her. Later, they exchanged letters—her letters full of remarkable perceptions—and Ernie found himself longing to see her again. The doctor encouraged the relationship—Ernie's friendship seemed to have a salutary effect on her condition—while warning Ernie not to let himself get too involved. The girl might improve, he told Ernie, but there would be inevitable relapses; she would never be able to lead a wholly normal life. Ernie threw himself headlong into the relationship with the girl and an odd turnabout took place. As the girl made an astonishing recovery, Ernie began drinking to excess, seemed to come apart. When the girl no longer needed him, she rejected Ernie for a man who seemed more confident of himself. After that Ernie went through a period of bad weather, was drunk more often than not and got into a succession of pointless brawls. Eventually, the experience toughened him, made him more attentive to the demands of self.

18

Women. That's another story, though also inextricably connected to the story of Ernest Sommer's rise and fall. At a certain point in his life, women became almost as crucial to Ernie as books. Their pursuit, their affection, their approval conferred status on him. He was suddenly important enough to be loved for reasons other than himself.

I remember a lunch we had together when all Ernie wanted to talk about was "this absolutely gorgeous lady" who had come to his office to interview him for some magazine. "I said to her," he told me, "that all she had to do was say the word and I'd run off with her to some edenic spot on the other side of the globe and she says, looking directly at me, and this is a gorgeous lady, What word is that, Mr. Sommer? I told her I was serious and she says, this dazzler, the kind of lady that never would have looked at me twice outside of this book-lined office, I think you're a beautiful man, Mr. Sommer."

"I said to myself she had to be kidding. Smart, I may be. Beautiful I ain't. But she meant it and after the interview was concluded—I mean she was there to do a job—she demonstrated her sincerity. You know what I'm saying?"

How could he continue living with one woman when almost every desirable woman he came in contact with was available to him. "I can't handle it," he said whenever the subject came up. It was more of a boast than a self-deprecation, though the remark was not without some regret.

19

Zoe put up with Ernie's womanizing for a time—he would get over it, she must have thought—but then they had a fight at a party over the attention Ernie paid some starlet or princess and everything that had been kept inside came out.

Ernie professed shock at Zoe's abrupt explosion. "How can someone you lived with for twelve years treat you that way?" was his constant question.

Whatever happened next happened quickly. Zoe moved out, took the child, accused Ernie of promiscuous adultery, and sued him for two thirds of his recorded income.

According to Jack, nothing hurt Ernie more than Zoe's disaffection. After she left him his confidence began to erode.

Ernie is reported to have thrown himself at Zoe's feet in the lobby of her apartment building in an attempt at reconciliation. He apparently begged her to come back to him, using all his powers of persuasion.

20

"He hated more than anything not to get his way," Zoe told us. "He absolutely refused being turned down, though he would say—it was one of his favorite lines—that he never wanted anything for himself, that he could survive on nothing if he had to.

"I told him several times to let go of my ankles, that he had no business keeping me from my appointment. When he released me, I said no hard feelings and walked out on him."

"You didn't kick him as he claims?"

"Kick him?" The question seems to amuse her. "I didn't kick him, if that's what he says—he would say that—which is to say it wasn't my intention to kick the son of a bitch. When I saw blood coming from his lip I felt awful, was ready to drop everything and look after him for as long as he needed me. I've always felt that way about Ernie. Let's just say that whatever happens, Ernie and I will always be friends."

"Did she really say that?" Ernie asked me. "That's unbelievable. That lady has class."

21

A former acquaintance of Ernie's, an author who had not written anything in years, showed up one morning at Ernie's door to accuse Ernie of having ruined his life. The man was unpleasant but also in need—broke and broken—so Ernie, who was temporarily living alone, let him stay over for a couple of nights. The former acquaintance read the gesture as an admission of Ernie's guilt and became even more demanding and abusive. It was the man's idea that Ernie was part of some kind of Jewish establishment that controlled who got published and who didn't. In his crazed view, Ernie had cut off all avenues of publication to him because he had once made an anti-Semitic remark in Ernie's presence. As a consequence of Ernie's perceived treachery, the man had lost the will to write. Although he despised the intruder,

Ernie suffered his extended visit, felt in some inexplicable way obligated to the man. The man became fixated with Ernie, dressed in his clothes, imitated his voice on the phone, wrote letters in which he signed himself Ernest Sommer. One night Ernie woke to see his other self lighting a fire in Ernie's bedroom. The attempted murder released Ernie from any feelings of obligation. He threw the man out of his apartment and then subdued the fire. Ernie was burned, we understand, though nothing serious.

Ernie thinks of himself as rising from the fire like a phoenix.

22

The day after Ernie separated from the publishing house he had imagined into existence, it was as if he had never been there. When I called to speak to him—it was how I had learned he had gone—his former employees seemed unable to remember his name.

I was shunted from receptionist to receptionist, was kept waiting for ten minutes, then found myself holding a dead phone. Ernie will be furious at such incompetence, I thought, or else get a good laugh out of it. Colonel Fiction, as we sometimes called him, tended to complain in a seemingly parodic way at the quality of the help. If the gossip can be believed, he once asked a pompous young editor to sweep out his office and polish his desk. The editor quit (a week after he had both swept and polished) and Ernie is reputed to have said, "If you can't last fifteen rounds, there's no point in fighting for the championship of the world."

The second time I phoned, some assistant told me that Ernie was no longer employed at Cervantes & Sons. I thought of saying that a company doesn't employ its owner, but let it pass. I asked to speak to one of the partners. Both were in conference at the moment and were not expected to

171

be free to come to the phone for an indefinite period of time. I left my name in that void, expecting it to disappear as heartlessly as Ernie had.

I called Ernie at home later that day and got no answer. And then, involved in my own work, I didn't concern myself with Ernie for a few days—maybe it was a few weeks—let the issue of his apparent disappearance slide. The next time I called his apartment his phone had been disconnected.

A few days after that, Jack told me Ernie had moved out of his loft and no one, at least no one Jack had talked to, knew where he had gone. Traces of him remained in the atmosphere like the fragments of an exploded meteor.

23

Time passes as we wait for Ernie to surface. Zoe publishes a novel centered around a character that resembles Ernie Sommer. This Ernie, called Howard Swift in the novel, is a heavy drinker and semi-heavy womanizer, a man unable to control the least of his desires. (By the time the book came out, Zoe had married her therapist from whom, one imagines, she had gotten her license to kill.) There is some sympathy for Howard/Ernie in the book, though it relies for the most part on the heroine's willful generosity, the object of it beyond redemption.

It was not a heroic portrait; it was not a portrait of the man we thought we knew as Colonel (sometimes Major, sometimes Captain) Fiction. Howard Swift is a nightclub comedian who becomes a talk show host, becoming more ruthless and exploitative (and sexually bizarre) with each new success.

"Perhaps it's not meant to be Ernie at all," Jack suggested. "The character of Howard Swift may have no prototype in the real world but chiche."

I wrote Zoe a long letter protesting the book's portrait of

172

Ernie, but then misplaced it among my papers or threw it out accidentally.

24

A story circulates—it is one rumor among many—that Ernie cut himself off from his old friends in order to pursue his own writing. I tend to accept rumors that have a poetic rightness about them even if their source is less than authoritative. I imagine Ernie writing in longhand on loose-leaf pages, working all day and into the night, drinking bourbon and pacing the room, an obsessive figure capable of the most extreme vices and the most intense virtue.

When will we hear from him again? I sit patiently at my desk and put down words, fragments, sentences, paragraphs in what seems to me a telling order. As I write, I glance over my shoulder from time to time (I'm speaking figuratively of course), looking for Ernie, imagining myself as Ernie, wanting to be greeted by my friends as I emerge from obscurity.

25

I am at my desk trying to imagine the next stage of Ernie's career, trying to create an imaginary history more substantial and valid than the real one. Who is Ernie after all?

There are a number of possible conclusions to his story, none absolutely right, almost all with some claim to verisimilitude. I put them down in longhand on the loose-leaf sheet in front of me.

A pseudonymous manuscript of over 1200 pages shows up (delivered by messenger) in the office of an editor of some power and authority. It is accompanied by a note from the reclusive writer, H, commending it to the editor. The book is published, gets mostly excellent if uncompre-

173

hending reviews, sells modestly, is almost sold to the movies. At some point Ernie lets out in an interview that he is the actual author.

Ernie produces a best seller of little or no literary value, talks in interviews about the importance of reaching a large audience. Established as a public figure, he laments the plight of celebrities, says all he wants is to be left alone to write his books.

Ernie reemerges as the editor-in-chief of a new incarnation of a once prestigious men's magazine, which in its bid for trendiness had lost its identity. He calls a press conference to announce that the magazine will publish the best writing in America and the world regardless of mass market appeal, that its only aim is to be first rate. The opening issue sells out; the second issue does almost as well; the third sells half as many as the second. Ernie leaves his post after ten months to write a memoir of the experience.

Unable to write at the level of his aspirations, Ernie gives way to depression, drinks heavily, turns himself into a clinic for rehabilitation, writes the story of his breakdown and recovery.

Ernie writes versions of the books he's admired, publishes them under pseudonyms, lives modestly out of the public eye. Most of us never see him again, though over drinks we share anecdotes about his career, keeping Ernie afloat in the collective imagination like a character in a novel.

THE ERRANT
MELANCHOLY
OF TWILIGHT

Some stories come on one like an unwelcome guest or a bad debt, engendering a sense of obligation toward them. One passes them on as a burden to be discharged. I dislike sentimentality and the story in point is nothing, reduces itself to small-minded irony, if not sentimental. A writer, then an ambitious fledgling of 18, falls in love with the heroine of a movie, or with the beautiful actress playing her, or with an idea of the actress playing the heroine, an adolescent infatuation with an image. The movie is called *Errant Melancholy* and is still shown on occasion for reasons that have little to do with the attractions of its heroine—the *Cahiers* critics admired its use of reverse tracking shots—in revival houses and college film series. Is it the role in the movie, a false and sentimental role, or is it the beauty of the actress that makes its indelible appeal on Harry Berger? It was not as though he ever expected anything from Norah Ashe, anything real or human. As long as she stayed as beautiful as she was, Berger would keep the faith, had kept it in fact, had let it lapse through two marriages and five prolonged love affairs.

Twenty-six years later, Berger met Norah Ashe at a cocktail party in another country. "I'm an admirer of your fiction," she said to him, as beautiful as she was, enhanced by the years. "Which fiction is that?" he quipped, frightened at her proximity. It was not that he hadn't met film stars before, it was just that he hadn't met this one, and this was the one that held top billing in one of the longest running of his fantasies. "Are you making fun of me, Mr. Berger?" she asked. The image on the screen was talking to him, her audience, without intercession of illusion. Nervousness disguised itself as familiarity. Berger confessed to having admired her as an actress, as an object of admiration, mentioned her first film, *Errant Melancholy*, the one that had won him. "Oh that," she said disparagingly. "Everyone fell in love with me in that." Although pained by her remark — if he was everyone, he was no one — he followed her across the room in the vain hope of recouping his losses.

He remembers thinking that she chattered to excess, was too conscious of her power to charm. Yet she was less vain, less narcissistic certainly, than most of the beautiful women he had known, and she was intelligent. In his journal Berger wrote:

> We got into a discussion about the fiction of M, which she thought inferior to mine for reasons that were exceptionally astute. I of course defended M against her criticisms.

2

Berger was surprised that she called him at his flat two days later, particularly so since he had not given out his number. Would he come to a dinner party she was giving on Saturday week? "I'd prefer to come over when no one else is there," he said.

His remark produced an awkward silence. "That wasn't very kind, was it?" she said. "What on earth does one do with a person like you?"

"I apologize if my remark seemed unkind to you," he said. "Unkindness was not in the least my intention."

3

"Our dialogue sounds like something out of one of your novels," she said.

"That's funny," he said. "I was going to say it sounded like something out of one of your lesser films."

4

It was one of those conversations in which everything he said was either miscalculated or misunderstood. Attempts at reparation only compounded the mischief. Berger seemed driven to destroy himself in her eyes, though he was trying, from all accounts, to make himself agreeable. At one point, at the height of his exasperation with himself, he said, "You can withdraw the invitation if you like. I'll understand." At another, he asked her if it was all right if he brought a companion.

"I don't think I've made myself clear," she said. "The companion you are being invited to bring is me."

"Now I really am embarrassed," Berger said. "I hope you won't hold our misunderstanding against me. I'm terrifically pleased to be invited to your party."

"Your reputation as a bounder precedes you, Mr. Berger."

He couldn't imagine it having been worse had he dreamed the encounter or invented it on the page.

5

Berger was ten days away from leaving London to return home, and in his head, if not heart, he was already in transit. He mentions the fact to indicate the unpremeditation of what happened next. Berger writes, "I thought of our meeting as a dispelling of illusion. One never wholly gets over one's first unconsummated romance."

In my own view, Berger is self-deceived as to what he wanted to happen at Norah's dinner party. His ambition was too large, too far-ranging, to let itself be constrained by rational considerations.

6

What struck him about the dinner party was that she never seemed to get the meal beyond its advance notice. "Are you people hungry?" Norah asked her five guests at a few minutes after nine o'clock and everyone except Berger, hungriest of all if it be known though on his best behavior, indicated a readiness to approach the dining table. It was as if the offer of food was the dinner itself. The conversation went on to something else, famine in Cambodia or the Chinese cinema or the most natural position for lovemaking. The English film producer was on his fourth Scotch while his actress wife, perhaps companion, was rolling marijuana cigarettes, four or five already in circulation. At twenty-five after nine, Norah, glancing in the direction of the kitchen, mentioned that dinner would be ready at any time. Ten o'clock arrived and nothing had come from the kitchen, not even the breeze of an aroma. Resisting whatever ironic remarks came to mind, Berger sat mute, sipping a '69 Margaux he had brought as a gift. From time to time he took a drag on the joint that passed his way, finding it more awkward to refuse than accept. The missing dinner, that failed promise, obsessed him like love denied. "Is there something I can do to help?" he asked his hostess, whom he had come to think of as mad. "Just stay as sweet as you are," said Norah. The other actress, an intense brunette some years younger than Norah, a woman named Jane, patted his hand, auditioned briefly for his affection. Her lover or husband took Berger aside to retail an unintelligible secret. The third man, an architect or musician named Norman, came over to say that he had once read a book of Berger's though couldn't recall the title. "It will come to me," he promised.

7

Berger sneaked a look at his digital watch. The watch, it might be said, winked back. Did no one else notice that it was approaching 10:30 and that dinner (the one they had all been invited to) had not been served? The film producer was dancing with the musician's wife to unheard music and Norah asked Berger if he would mind terribly dancing with her. "Could we wait for something slower to come on," he said. "This music's a little fast for me."

"We're all a little fast for you here," she said, "aren't we? I'll bet we are. We can dance at whatever speed you like. The music's barely audible so one can't hold it responsible, can one? You lead, Mr. Berger, and I'll follow."

The prospect of dancing with her frightened him, threatened the dissolution of his fantasy. "I'll lead you wherever you want to go," he said, "within reason."

"Is reason going to get in our way?" she asked, this more than beautiful woman. "The presupposition of your work is that you're anything but a reasonable man."

The conversation led everywhere yet Berger uncharacteristically declined to pursue the question obsessing him, said nothing about the unarrived dinner. The perfume in her hair intoxicated him. "What do you say, sweetheart," he whispered in uncertain imitation of Humphrey Bogart, "we go out somewhere and catch a bite."

She stopped dancing abruptly. "What time is it?" she demanded, as if he were personally responsible for the lateness of the hour.

"It's not so late," he said, protecting her from the news he had been commanded to report.

"I should get the dinner on the table, shouldn't I? Do you think the others are hungry?"

"I don't mean to be impertinent, Norah, but is there really a dinner being prepared?"

"You *do* mean to be impertinent," she said, as if impertinence were an ingratiating quality. "Did you think I would invite people to dinner and not offer them anything to eat? Did you really think that, Mr. Berger?"

"I confess the idea occurred to me," he said, "though I expected whatever you did you would do with appropriate style."

"It's a cold dinner, fresh vegetables and an aioli sauce, so it doesn't need any real preparation. I'll serve it this instant if you want me to."

He was enjoying the closeness the dance afforded and was reluctant, hungry as he was, to relinquish it for something as unnourishing as food.

"A good hostess tends to anticipate the wishes of her guests," she said, "wouldn't you say? We might go on a tour of the house first and then eat."

Berger laughed, assuming a joke. "Won't your other guests feel left out?" he asked.

Her face froze, though his vantage as dancing partner precluded such recognition.

"Do you want them to join us?" she whispered. "Is that your pleasure?"

In his day, which was but in its early afternoon, Berger was known to be game for anything. Nevertheless, her suggestion, if he understood it correctly, shocked him mildly. "I'd prefer a private tour," he said.

"We're famished, Norah," the producer, whose name was Lord something, called to them. "Give us a break, love."

"In a minute, Larry," she said. "Why don't you have a wee Scotch while I get myself together?"

Norah led him into the kitchen where a servant, head pressed to the table, slept like a child, and into a room beyond, furnished as a study. She closed the door between the two rooms, latched it from the inside. "I've got you now, Mr. Berger," she said.

8

He never expected that his fantasies would find precise correlation in the real world, though did what he could to overfill the imagination. Real life was what he did between novels. Norah observed him with a cool smile, a woman passionate in her detachments. She took his hand, held it at her side, brought it to her mouth, tongue scorching his palm. Although impressed by her beauty, perhaps in awe of it, he felt no urgency about lying down with her on the plush velvet couch at the far end of the room. Mostly he was curious as to what might happen next. "Am I a satisfactory hostess, Mr. Berger?" she asked.

"I find it exciting to be called, Mr. Berger," he said.

After they kissed she said, "To be frank, Mr. Berger, I'm not into kissing all that much. Do you mind?"

At dinner—it was finally served at five minutes to midnight—Berger found it unimaginable that he had just moments before made love to Norah Ashe in her study. He admired her sangfroid before and after, was dazzled by it, felt awkward and graceless in comparison. There had been so little acknowledgement of feelings that he had no idea what it had meant to her or even, come down to it, what it meant to himself. Nothing was ever quite real to him—a professional hazard perhaps—without language to give it definition.

9

If the wait for dinner seemed inordinate, the wait for the party's conclusion seemed in the endless anticlimatic repetitions a stay against aging and death. At three A.M., the party as lively or deadly as it had ever been (the producer was retailing a long anecdote about a famous bisexual star that promised some flash of wit at the conclusion that never arrived), Berger announced that it was time for him to go, standing on legs that had only the barest recollection of the processes of locomotion.

"Must you run off?" said a woman named Glynnis who had hardly spoken to him before. "We were just getting to know you."

Norah took his hand in her proprietary way and conducted him to the door. Berger fought back a yawn which asserted itself the moment he thought he had beaten it down. "We've tired you out, I see," she said.

"It happens to be past my bedtime," he said.

"How quaint," she said. "I thought you American writers stayed up around the clock, drinking and brawling and that sort of thing. Is it that you go to lengths to avoid cliché? Has anyone ever told you . . . but I won't say it." Her smile was as dazzling as ever, was irresistible.

He didn't ask for the completion of the sentence, said he would call her tomorrow, aware inescapably of the parodic aspect of the remark.

"Of course you will," she said, squeezing his hand before returning it to him. Am I a disappointment? her eyes seemed to ask. He had no way of answering her unspoken question, or he would hold on to his answer for an appropriate occasion, would nurture it into eloquence.

10

It was his curse to be moved more by the imagination of something, by its unbidden recollection, than by the experience itself. He did everything he could to live in the present short of succeeding at it, pursued the moment whatever dark place it would take him, at best a fraction of a second behind. It was as though he had to know what he knew, to see it on the page before his eyes—the mysterious authority of the written word—to make it real as experience. He had no life, had barely breathed the air, until he translated it into language. Aware of this failing, he refused to write about Norah in his journal, sat staring at the blank page in an agony of denial.

If she didn't answer by the fifth ring, he decided, he would relinquish his quest, take a hot bath, read a book, and with any luck get four or five hours sleep.

On the sixth ring she answered in an uncharacteristic mumble.

"Norah?"

"Yes?"

"It's Harry Berger."

"I know who it is. Would you be a love and call back in the morning?"

"The others are still there?"

"We'll talk tomorrow morning if that suits you. All right?"

"I work in the mornings," he said. "I'll call you when I break for lunch."

"That will be delightful," she said.

11

Berger did no work in the morning. He slept fitfully until ten-thirty, woke in a state of uncharacteristic self-loathing. He tended, like the various protagonists of his fiction, barely disguised projections of himself, to obsessive behavior. It was childlike he knew, or allowed himself to know when the obsession had passed, to insist on having the very thing he wanted (no displacements, no substitutes) the very instant he wanted it. On the other hand, he was essentially a passive man, a flag in the wind.

He decided not to call her back, not right away, not as if he had to (as he had to), so he went out at noon to avoid temptation, took a walk on the heath. His life at times seemed like a novel by someone wholly unlike himself, full of significances disguised in circumstantiality. The Hampstead Everyman was showing *Errant Melancholy*—he noticed a poster for it in a butcher's window—that very afternoon. The timing had a dreamlike appropriateness. He had the idea of inviting Norah to see the revival with him, though ended up going alone. It was his *Errant Melancholy* he was going to see, not hers. At worst it might cure him, if from what he suffered was susceptible to remedy.

The movie was not as different from his recollections of it as he had prepared himself to anticipate. Norah Ashe played an orphaned mute of about 16 or 17 apprenticed to a morose clown in an itinerant circus. The clown abuses Norah—he tends to express his affection in negative gestures—though is well-intentioned by his own dim lights. On her part, Norah is all innocence and good faith. DeFlores teaches her his routines, beating Norah for each mistake, and shortly the pupil is a more accomplished performer than the master, more delicate and subtle, more finely tuned. An impressario for a great circus catches one of Norah's performances and comes to her tent afterward to offer her a job in the big time. When Norah realizes that the offer precludes DeFlores she rejects it without telling her master either of the offer or of her refusal of it.

Aware that he is losing his touch, DeFlores begins to drink heavily. When drunk he is pathologically brutal. At one point, out of misguided jealousy, he slaps Norah repeatedly across the face, unable to stop himself, until it enlists from his protégée the first word we have heard her speak, "Don't." DeFlores is moved by her triumph and falls to his knees, embracing her feet.

After an interlude in which he is loving and kind to her, DeFlores is heckled by an obnoxious audience and drinks himself into a murderous rage. Frightened for her life Norah flees the circus and finds herself alone on the road with no idea where to go. After a succession of travails—attempted rape, near starvation, suicidal despair—the impressario discovers her sitting forlornly at the edge of a river. Norah joins the big circus and in seemingly record time becomes an international star. Eventually, the handsome impressario proposes marriage, but Norah refuses him, indicating that she is committed to someone else.

The film cuts away to DeFlores who is still employed by the same small traveling circus. Word gets back to him that Norah, under another name, is performing with the Grand International Circus encamped in the center of the city some fifteen miles away from his ragtag outfit. It is a hot summer day and DeFlores, still wearing his clown makeup, sets off on foot to reclaim Norah. The Grand International Circus is giving a command performance for some visiting royalty and as DeFlores strides across the countryside, cannons go off in symbolic tribute. He finds Norah in her dressing room, putting on her clown face. When she sees him, she whispers his name then collapses in a faint. In the next shot we see DeFlores walking through a field carrying Norah in his arms, the hot sun beating down on his bare head, his face a mask of anguish. DeFlores' knees buckle on several occasions, but out of implacable will he retains his balance. The sun blinds him. He hallucinates a scene from earlier in the film where they perform together as clowns. The applause thunders in the distance. After a while, DeFlores collapses under the burden of Norah's weight and the blinding heat of the sun. Norah falls across his chest. The reality that survives—DeFlores' last fleeting perception before darkness overtakes him—is of the two of them performing together to

185

cheering crowds. Norah mouths the words, "I love you," DeFlores pretending not to notice, though his face, the face of the dying clown, is illumined by that perception.

11

Berger walked under the remorseless London sun from his flat in Hampstead to her house in Chelsea, feeling not unlike the aging clown in the film. He went into a phone box to warn her of his imminent appearance—he was after all a temperate, reasonable man—but after getting a busy signal, he decided to keep the integrity of his gesture intact.

If he wore a hat, if he had ever worn one, he would have arrived holding it in hand. "Do with me what you will," he might have said, but he didn't talk that way, was too sophisticated, had too much self-control.

A servant let him in, the one he had seen sleeping in the kitchen the night before. Norah was at the shops, she said, would return at any time. Did he care to wait?

Berger looked at the paintings on the living room wall, a Chagall, an Avery, a Sickert, a Klee drawing, an over-finished portrait of Norah in the manner (though without the brash skill) of Augustus John. The servant returned to ask if Berger would like some tea.

Did she have any idea when Norah might return? The question elicited the same answer he had gotten before. Miss Ashe had gone to the shops and was expected to return at any time.

The English, in his experience, never answered the questions addressed to them, withheld the most commonplace information as if they were protecting national secrets.

"Will she be back within an hour?"

"I really couldn't say."

Berger stayed another ten minutes then got up to go, said to tell Norah that Harry Berger had dropped by. The woman gave him a piece of paper on which to write down his name. He wrote, DeFlores.

Berger walked over to Kings Road, looked in the window of two or three shops, then took a cab to his flat on Downshire Hill.

A woman was coming toward the cab as he emerged from it, taking possession (as he perceived it in slow motion) of everything in her path. She put an arm on his shoulder. They went inside, went immediately, unhesitatingly to bed. He had the feeling he had been chosen for some sort of national honor. "It was like being knighted," he wrote in his journal.

Afterward she said, "I was very angry with you last night, and I doubt that you have the faintest idea why."

"I wasn't supposed to leave the party until you dismissed me."

She laughed in excess of the provocation. "I do think we might get along after all," she said. Then: "Am I really so imperious? I want the unvarnished truth."

13

"Am I really so imperious?"

He knew the question was a trap, though couldn't resist an answer. "Being with you is like having an audience with the queen," he said.

She showed her displeasure by stamping her foot. "I don't think you really understand women," she said. "Your books are a great dodge."

"No doubt you're right. You have the advantage, of course, of your own example."

"I'm easy to understand, child's play. If I may say so, I think you try too hard."

"Off with my head."

"Precisely."

187

14

Berger returned to the states and picked up his life, fell into old routines, felt displaced. Writing fiction was what he did between forays in the real world. He was at the house in New Hampshire on the third beginning of a new book, a novella dealing with obsessive jealousy. A young woman named Kiki came with him—he didn't like to be completely cut off—but after two weeks he sent her packing. Her presence irritated him (like some unaccountable urban hum) and he found he couldn't work with her in the same house. A week later, lonely and disheartened, he called Kiki and asked her if she would like to come up for the weekend. She said she might come though wasn't sure, couldn't and wouldn't promise. He said to do as she liked, that he would not expect her but would be pleased at her arrival.

Afterward, confident of her return, disinterested in it, he suffered briefly the anxiety of excessive self-esteem. He had asked Kiki to return because he thought he owed her the opportunity to reject him. It was not his fault she was in thrall to him. His triumph, if that's what it was (a recent pattern in his life), staled almost immediately.

15

What they had in common, he and Norah, was a species of unillusionment. They had no need for coyness or the trappings of self-justifying romance. Berger was tired of living with women who admired him to death and waited on him and did, to a point, whatever he asked of them. Such relationships were without mystery, engendered a certain complacency. On the other hand, he and Norah were equals, both artists with serious, important careers, both mature and experienced—she perhaps more experienced even than he. One doesn't think: It is time to leave childishness behind. One merely attempts to escape certain patterns of the past only to meet them again in new disguise.

16

Berger dreamed that Norah Ashe was making a movie of *Antony and Cleopatra*, and he began to think of her as his illicit queen, his temptress, his princess of Eros, his Nile.

17

He wrote to Norah inviting her to come and stay with him in the house in New Hampshire as soon as she was clear of professional commitments, a hardheaded letter that never once, not even in its closing, mentioned the word love. When he no longer expected an answer—six weeks had passed without word—a telegram arrived indicating the time of her arrival at Logan Airport in Boston. In the meantime he had the unenviable task of gently dispatching Harriet Barr who was doing a Ph.D. thesis on him and had come all the way from Mill Valley, California to do her research firsthand.

18

Berger remembers how jittery he was waiting for Norah at the airport, how he paced the waiting room like some Hollywood idea of an expectant father. Her plane was delayed and he remembers fixing on the idea that she is not on the plane, that she has changed her mind.

His dignity is a sham, is in shambles, but he works at it, receives her with a diplomat's solemnity. "Welcome to my country," he wants to say both seriously and in parody.

She is tired and irritable, treats him not as Antony but as one of the household slaves. That night in a hotel room he will say, "My asp is at your service."

189

"For God's sake don't look at me," she says in the morning, covering her face with her hands.

At her whim they stay another day at the hotel, postponing the visit to his house in New Hampshire. "I don't know how to do without creature comforts," she warns him. "I think if one can afford to live with some style and elegance, one ought not to shirk that opportunity."

"I lead a rather ascetic life," he tells her. "I write every day or almost every day. Unless I get a minimum of four hours in, my hand shakes."

"Does it? I have absolutely no intention of trying to compete with your work." She made up her face in the mirror over the dresser, taking twice the time she ordinarily took. "I'm a creature of routines as you can see. It may seem like vanity to you, but it's a professional necessity to me."

20

After spending two weeks with him in the house in New Hampshire, Norah let it be known one afternoon — they had picnicked on the grounds of a deserted estate down the road — that she was to leave for Los Angeles in three days to start work on a film. It was the first Berger had heard of the commitment, and he assumed that Norah was using it as an occasion to dissolve the present arrangement. He acknowledged her decision without argument or complaint, said he would drive her to the airport in Boston when she was ready to go.

Later, she said, "I didn't mean to break the news to you so abruptly, Harry. I just didn't know how else to get it said." They were sitting in front of the fireplace, her head against his shoulder.

"You knew what you were doing," he said.

"You *are* angry at me, aren't you? Well, you shouldn't be, you really shouldn't. I accepted the part, which I think is a challenging one by the way, over a month ago. I wouldn't have accepted it if I didn't think it was something important for me. You have to trust that."

He made a conscious decision not to press her to change her mind, said he valued her commitment to her work, but he was disappointed, as she might expect, at losing her company.

"You could come with me if you like. I know you don't like southern California much, but I could show it to you in a way you haven't seen it before."

The idea recommended itself briefly. "I won't reject it out of hand," he said, "though I've never figured out what 'out of hand' actually means. Out of whose hand?"

"It means rejecting it before you've held on to it for a while, before you've really touched it."

"How do you know that?"

"It stands to reason, doesn't it? Do come with me, Harry. Do."

If he went with her to California, he would be in the odious role of camp follower, a role that invited humiliation. Of greater or lesser concern, he would be in danger of losing the thread of the book he was on. Berger shook his head. Had she really wanted him to come, he decided, she would not have created a situation that engendered resistance. She was much too subtle for that, much too careful about getting her way.

"Think about it," she said.

21

After he took Norah to the airport he had dinner in Cambridge with some old friends, George and Anne Cooper, both of them writers a long time between books.

191

"What is Norah Ashe really like?" Anne asked him over dinner.

"She's painfully shy and withdrawn," Berger said, "sits in the corner much of the day sucking her thumb." George, who was a receptive audience, laughed.

"You're making that up," Anne said. "Aren't you?"

"You're on to me," he said. "The truth is, she's an engine of sexual excess and depravity. She sits in the corner much of the day sucking my thumb."

Anne kept after him. "Is she as beautiful in real life as she is on the screen?"

"She carries a steamer trunk full of makeup with her wherever she goes," Berger said. "I've never seen her without her mask."

"Are you being serious?"

"I'm making this up," he said. "In point of fact, Norah Ashe is imaginary. We lead a quiet imaginary life together."

22

Sometimes Berger felt as if he had imagined himself. Norah called from a hotel in Santa Monica and said she missed him.

"I've been missing," he admitted.

"I can't hear you," she said. "The connection's bad."

The connection was fine on his end. He heard what sounded like drunken voices in the background and could imagine a party he was glad to have avoided.

"I've missed you too," he said. "My life has been uneventful without you."

"I hope you've written thousands of pages in my absence."

"The truth is, I've reworked the same page close to a thousand times. After a point, I give it up and start over. I'm more productive with you here than with you gone."

He waited for her to renew her invitation to California, prepared to reject it again, but she didn't make it, and he felt the loss.

"Give me a number where I can reach you," he said. "I'll call the next time."

"Do you know," she said, "I've found a copy of your first novel, and I've been reading it every night before going to sleep. How old you were, how old and wise!"

The compliment touched him to embarrassment. "Everyone fell in love with me in that," he said.

"Yes," she said. "They did and still do."

23

Berger woke up one morning with an idea for a short story. A lonely man imagines himself living with the heroine of a film (or of a novel), imagines that she is not the fictional character but a real-life counterpart from whom the character is all too literally drawn. He enters the fiction (or film) himself and extends it by living out a narrative with its heroine, becoming himself the hero of the film (or fiction), ultimately falling victim to the tragic outcome he imagines for the work (film or novel), his concern with form (as artist) taking priority over the will to survive.

24

Berger phoned his agent in New York and asked if the man who had taken an option on his last novel, a man he had previously refused to meet, would be willing to fly him out to California for a consultation.

The agent, a dour man given to no easy optimism, said he would look into it, would call him back as soon as he had an answer.

"Shall I tell him you'll consider doing a screenplay?"

Berger needed no time to consider the question. "Not if my life depended on it, Alex. Not if your life depended on it."

"I'll do my best," Alex said, "not to discourage the man beyond repair."

25

Harriet Barr was difficult to discourage and Berger, going through a period of self-doubt, lacked the motivation to run her off. He found her an ambiguous consolation, full of unanswerable questions and heart-rending gestures.

"You're my idol," she told him under the gun. "If I were a male, I'd want to grow up to be you."

He was as kind to her as unwarranted sovereignty permitted.

26

"How's the motion picture business?" he asked.

"Disastrous," she said. "I've written you a longish letter with all the sordid and squalid details. Suffice to say, if I knew then what I know now, I would be in New Hampshire with you this very moment."

"How much longer will you have to be there, Norah?"

"It's impossible to say. We're already two, maybe three, weeks behind schedule. If I could get out of my contract, darling, I'd fly to Boston at first opportunity."

"It's possible that I may have to go to Los Angeles myself for a few days on some business."

"That would be lovely, though do try to come before we go on location in New Mexico. Excuse me. Someone's at the door, Harry. I'll call you back as soon as I get free. Will you be there?"

"There's nowhere else to go," he said.

194

By the time Berger had his all-expenses-paid invitation to go to California, Norah was on location in New Mexico.

Instead of going to Los Angeles, Berger went on a goodwill tour to the Soviet Union with two poets, an aging dancer, and a former book editor of *The New York Times*.

He was introduced at a conference in Kiev as the husband of the great theatrical artist, Norah Ashe. It was the first time their names had been coupled in any country.

"If I wanted to be ironic with you," Berger said, "I might say that Norah Ashe and I are just good friends. As it is, we are barely acquaintances. I've always wondered how such unfounded rumors achieve credence." The audience, in response to what may have been a distorted translation of his remarks, laughed and applauded.

28

Berger hated literary gossip, particularly when it involved him, loathed having his private life deformed into public spectacle. So when the former book editor of *The New York Times* confessed that it was he who had mentioned Berger's name in conjunction with Norah Ashe to one of the Russians, Berger was furious.

"All I said, Harry, was that I thought the two of you made a particularly distinguished couple."

"If you ever do anything like that again, Lionel," Berger said out of the side of his mouth, "I'll take out a full page ad in *The New York Times* to tell everyone who doesn't already know what a horse's ass you are."

"Do you have any idea what those ads cost?" the former editor said. "That's the most flattering threat I've ever received. Tell me something, Harry—what's the real story? Rumor has it that you and Norah have gone splitsville."

If he wasn't a pacifist and didn't have a bad back and wasn't in a foreign country Berger might have taken the measure of the former book editor. As it was, he turned his back on the other and walked away.

29

She said it first. "I believe our names have coupled more in the past two months than we have."

"That's the power of the written word," Berger said.

On her second stay in new Hampshire, Norah was less demanding and self-willed. It was as though her first visit were a rehearsal in which everything that couldn't be used in performance had to be gotten out of the way.

Sometimes he was even secretly pleased to see his name appear with hers, if only to validate a reality he found difficult to credit.

His celebrity, which he found disturbing in direct proportion to the unadmitted pleasure it gave him, belonged to some other Harry Berger, a name he read about that happened circumstantially to be his own. A Jewish prince from Riverdale, fourth outfielder on his high school baseball team, editor of the yearbook, grows up to be a world-famous writer and the lover of a beautiful and gifted actress he used to fantasize about as an 18-year-old. Such facts had no relation to the real story. He was an artist first, a serious man, and only incidentally a public figure. Some tragedy or pathos awaited him.

30

Berger/DeFlores was trudging barefoot over mountainous terrain, bareheaded under the hottest of suns, soles of feet cut and bleeding, strength depleted by the overwhelming heat. What if she hadn't fainted, what if she had said, Look I'm not going with you, DeFlores, my career is more important to me—my art, she might have said— than whatever used to be between us, more brutality than affection if I remember correctly.

DeFlores, incapable of being rebuffed, as implacable as a force of nature, lifts her into his arms and carries her away, despite her struggles.

"Say something at least," she might have said, wanting him to acknowledge his love for her, to give it the solidity and abstraction of language.

Her request seems to surprise him. Wasn't he taking enormous risks to come after her in the enemy camp, the possibilities of humiliation and rejection at every turn? It was all he could do to carry her back in the insufferable heat. Wasn't the gesture enough, wasn't it everything?

"I am saying it," he said. "It's you who don't know how to listen."

31

She caught him one morning staring at her in sleep. "What's going on?" she asked. "Say something lovely to me, will you?"

Such requests tended to invite silence.

Norah returns his affectionate stare with only the barest hint of performance behind it.

I am in the wrong movie, Berger thinks, if he thinks anything at this moment, am fortuitously miscast in a sentimental melodrama with the texture of an adolescent's daydream.

My life is tragic, he wants to say, though with comic elements.

He performs his role as if he were born to it. Who's to know the imposture he thinks, if no one gives him away.

"I love you, Norah," he confided.

"And I have always loved you," she said in that marvelous voice that precluded disbelief.

Berger collapses under the combined oppression of her weight and the blinding heat of the sun. He falls.